ScorpionCay

By

Bill Craig

A Sam Decker Mystery

Dedication:

To my good friend Mary Anderson for
reminding me to
   Laugh at myself even during tough times.
   And to my son Jack who will always be a
source of both
   Laughter and Inspiration....

Chapter One

It was a typically warm balmy night in the Florida
Keys. A cool sea breeze was blowing in from the west,
carrying the scent of saltwater from the gulf in over the
island. A full moon had arisen white and bloated over the
horizon, glaring down from the night sky like a benevolent
eye of god. Russell Cosgrove sat on the patio of his beach
house looking out at the thin white foam from the breakers
where the waves were hitting the beach.

From inside the house he could hear the strains of
island jazz playing on the stereo. His girlfriend, Jessica
Monroe had delivered a frozen margarita to him just
moments before. He sipped at the drink, letting the alcohol
wash some of the salt from the rim of the glass into his

mouth as the breeze ruffled his long brown hair. He sighed contentedly. It was nice to be back from the hustle and grind of Miami. Nothing had looked as good to him as the sight of the ferry at the dock on Key West that would carry him back home to Scorpion Cay.

His law practice was doing well, so well in fact he had recently promoted three new partners in the firm to full partners. The added capital from their investments had put Cosgrove, Marshall, and Wilkes into new offices in downtown Miami. The glass-fronted high-rise dominated the downtown area, towering over all the other buildings in the area.

Some of the new clients that the new partners had brought with them had not thrilled him, however, that was business. As a lawyer he didn't have to approve of his clients, just represent them and their interests to the best of his abilities.

"Russ, how about we go over to the Parrot's Beak for karaoke tonight?" Jessica suggested as she stepped out onto the patio. She had a bottle of Miller's Genuine Draft beer in her hand. He turned and watched her as she tilted the bottle to her lips and drank the golden colored beer. It amazed him sometimes that she had fallen for him. At twenty-five, Jessica was less than half his age, but was still a considerable number of years younger than his own fifty-five years. Yet she seemed happy to be with him. He watched as she brushed back a strand of long blonde hair that the breeze had blown across her face. Standing there in the doorway, she had never, he thought, looked more beautiful.

"That sounds like fun, Jess. I had a pretty long day today in court and am worn out. Why don't you go ahead though? Just because I'm tired doesn't mean you can't go and have some fun," Russell told her. He felt himself smile as he took another drink of his margarita. Jimmy Buffet sure had the drinks pegged when he had penned the song *Margaritaville* all those years ago.

"Are you sure you don't mind, Russ?" she asked, walking over to stand beside him. Jessica leaned down over him, her breasts brushing his chest as she kissed him. "I could stay and give you a great back rub, or front rub," she told him with a smile, letting her hand rub through the thick carpet of hair on his tanned chest.

"That is almost too tempting an offer to pass up, Babe. Seriously though, I just want to sit back and unwind from the day. The Contras merger has me drained. So go sing and have fun," he replied smiling at her.

"You are working way too hard, Russ. If the merger

is taking that much out of you, why not delegate it to one of the junior partners?" she asked, concern audible in her voice. It gave him a warm feeling, hearing the tone in her voice. Just one more indication that the feelings they shared were real.

"Because Jerry Contras was my very first client when I opened my office. He's not comfortable with any of the associates. He also happens to be my oldest friend. So when he asked me to handle it, I couldn't say no," Russell explained.

"In other words, it's a guy thing. That old brotherhood sort of bond," Jessica replied with a sparkle in her eye.

"Yep. Exactly. A purely sexist macho type deal. So, are you going to sing in your bikini or actually wear clothing when you go to the Parrot's Beak?" Russ grinned.

"Well if I wear the bikini, nobody will realize how bad a voice I have," Jessica smiled back.

"Nonsense, Babe, you have a voice as lovely as a nightingale. They might think they have died and gone to heaven though, after hearing that voice and seeing such a heavenly body," Russell said with a smile.

"You definitely get a kiss for that comment," Jessica replied leaning over and pressing her body against him and slipping her hand behind his head, pulling his lips against hers. The kiss was long and passionate, and when it ended they were both breathing heavily. "Still want me to go?" she asked, her voice husky.

"I'm sure I'll regret this later, but yeah. Making love to you here on the beach right now would be wonderful, but I'm too tired to make it good for you," he replied sorrowfully.

"Hon, you always make it good for me, tired or not. Russell, you're the best lover I have ever had. There's also the fact that I love you, which also adds to it. So never doubt yourself on that score," Jessica told him.

"Point taken, Jessica. Are you certain you've never been a lawyer?" he asked with a grin.

"Positive, but I am shamelessly in love with one. Does that count?" she asked, grinning back.

"Yes, I believe it does. It counts for a lot with me," Russell told her. "Go get ready for karaoke. Have a great time."

"Only because you are insisting on it," Jessica laughed as she took another long pull on her beer. Flashing him a smile she walked into the house. Russell eased back in his chair after watching her go inside. Jessica was a special woman. Everyone who had met Jessica realized it, except maybe her. Jess was very self-depreciating and humble. Russell took another gulp of his margarita and leaned back in the chair. He would go in for another in a few minutes. For the moment, he was more than content to sit and enjoy the breeze.

Jessica drained her beer as she passed through the kitchen. She paused only long enough to drop the empty bottle in the trash before heading down the hall to the bedroom that she shared with Russell. He had been so wonderful since they had met two years before. He also encouraged her to continue writing and working on her novel. Russell was the first man she had ever met who understood her need to pursue her dream of writing. He had been a customer in the diner where she waited tables to support herself while she worked on her book.

She felt herself smile when she thought of her novel that way. Since meeting Russell, her writing had gotten better and she had re-written the story about four times and was finally getting deeper into it, understanding the characters with a stronger emotional connection that was coming through in the words. They were actually evoking emotions in her as she wrote them. It was some of the best work she had ever done in her life. Jessica smiled.

She wished that Russell knew how much he had inspired her. Quickly she stripped off her bikini and pulled out a pair of cotton briefs and stepped into them. A bra wasn't really much of a concern here in the Keys. She pulled out a sundress and pulled it over her head. Sandals followed, and then she headed for the bathroom to do her make-up. Twenty minutes later she was ready and heading back down the hallway towards the kitchen. Russell was pouring himself another margarita from the pitcher she had left in the fridge.

"Are you sure you won't reconsider and join me?" she asked him one more time. Going to karaoke was fun, but she enjoyed it so much more when she had him to sing to.

"I'm sure Jessica. One more of these and I may go ahead and slip off to bed. However, I will be rested by the time you get home so do feel free to wake me up," Russell replied with a grin.

"That's a promise, Lover," She told him, smiling back. Then she slipped into his arms, enjoying the warmth of his body as he held her tight. He leaned his face down to hers and they kissed again. It always amazed her how just his touch could send electric tingles through her body and cause her heartbeat to race. Finally the kiss ended.

"Later," she whispered softly as he released her.

"Count on it," he replied with a smile. He turned and walked back out onto the patio. Smiling, Jessica grabbed her purse from the kitchen counter and walked out the front door. She looked at the two vehicles sitting there. One was a BMW; the car that Russell always used to commute to Miami in, the other was an old jeep that they used whenever they were just driving around on the island. As lovely as the night was, it was definitely a Jeep night, she decided. She climbed into the Jeep and cranked the engine. It caught smoothly. Still smiling as she thought about Russell, she slipped the gearshift into reverse and backed out of the driveway. A moment later she was heading across the island to The Parrot's Beak.

Russell listened until the sound of the Jeep's engine had faded off into the distance. He hadn't wanted to tell her about the things he had discovered while working on the Contras merger. Hell, he hadn't even wanted to tell Jerry about it. However he knew that his client and friend needed to know the information. Russell had made sure that the accountants had double-checked the figures, but the numbers had come out the same. Someone was stealing from Contras manufacturing, and the company he was merging with wasn't in much better shape. Cosgrove knew

he would need to hire at least one, if not two investigators

to look into the embezzlement going on in both companies.

There were a lot of investigators available in

Miami, but they were not people that he had a great deal of

confidence in. No, he wanted an investigator that he knew

he could trust. He felt himself grin as he thought of the

perfect man for the job. The guy had an office and home

right on Scorpion Cay.

Sam Decker would be perfect for the job. He had

spent several years as an agent for the Drug Enforcement

Administration before pulling the plug and citing burnout

as the reason. Cosgrove knew the real reason was that

Decker had gotten tired of the corruption that came from

the ungodly amounts of money that was a by-product of the

drug trade. Decker had made a lot of enemies because he

was a straight arrow, intent on doing the job and he couldn't

be bought off or scared off.

There had been rumors about Decker that he

occasionally bent the rules or took shortcuts to make the

busts, but they were never proven as facts. Decker also

had a reputation as a bulldog. When he started on a case,

he would not let go until it was broke. Decker had a lot

of complaints of unnecessary force against him, but every

arrest he had made stuck. Yes, Sam Decker was the perfect choice. Hell, they had known each other for years. He scribbled the name down on a legal pad next to the deck chair. He leaned back and sipped more of his drink. The CD he had been listening to ended and the next one, a collection of sax jazz called of all things; Safe Sax, started playing.

Cosgrove leaned back in his chair. He took another drink, feeling the inner warmth from the frozen drink fill his belly. Much as he loved Jessica and loved being with her, he still needed some occasional downtime. Nights like tonight. Leaning back, his eyes closed, the soft music playing in the background, Russell Cosgrove didn't hear the approach of stealthy footsteps across the beach.

The man had slipped out of the water fifty yards or so down the beach, circling around through the mangrove jungle that flanked Russell Cosgrove's house. He was well prepared for his work, dressed in black battle dress utilities, a pistol was holstered on a belt at his waist, a submachine gun hung suspended from a sling across his shoulder. Tight leather gloves covered his hands, and his face was covered by a black baklava. Black jungle boots covered his feet, the Panama sole making distinct prints in the sand.

The rustle of the wind through the trees helped cover any incidental noise he might have made as he passed through the trees and bushes. The man moved closer to the house, pressing his back to it to peer around the corner and make sure he had not been spotted by the target. The target, Russell Cosgrove was sitting on the patio in a deck chair, some sort of drink in his hand. The assassin grinned beneath the black spandex mask that covered his face. Music drifted out of the house. Good, all the better to cover his approach. The assassin slipped around the house and let the sub gun fall on the sling. He reached down and drew the pistol, taking a suppressor from another pouch on the holster and screwed it into the pistol's muzzle.

A board creaked under his foot. Cosgrove leaned forward and turned his head, alerted by the sound. The assassin stabbed the silenced pistol forward just as Cosgrove was starting to speak. There was a flash from the muzzle of the pistol, a sound like a quiet cough. Russell Cosgrove fell out of the chair, the top half of his head missing. Blood immediately began pooling on the boards and dripping through the cracks between them. The killer moved back off the patio and faded away into the darkness, his job done.

Three hours later, Jessica Monroe pulled back into the driveway. She was staggering slightly as she climbed out of the Jeep. The Parrot's Beak had been a blast. She had even managed to win the singing contest with a heartfelt rendition of Janis Joplin's classic Mercedes Benz. There had been some tough competition though. She knew Russell would be proud of her. Stumbling to the door, she realized that the lights were all still on.

"Russell? Are you still up?" she called as she stepped inside the front door. There was no answer. Maybe he had fallen asleep outside. It wouldn't be the first time, she thought to herself with a grin. Jessica dropped her keys and purse on the kitchen counter as she walked through, heading for the patio door. She looked out the door. It looked like he was lying on the deck. Jessica slid the screen door open and stepped outside.

"Russell, wake up Hon. I'm horny and ready for you Lover," she said, walking towards him. Then she noticed the dark puddle around his head. Her first thought was that he had collapsed and cracked his head when he fell. Then she noticed that part of his head was missing. Jessica Monroe began to scream.

Chapter Two

The crunch of tires on gravel outside drew him instantly awake from a sound sleep. Sam Decker tossed off the light cotton sheet and rolled to his feet as his hand wrapped around the butt of his Sig-Saur P-228 9mm auto-loading pistol. His thumb had found the safety and clicked it off as he padded silently to the window on bare feet. Red and blue lights flashed through the blinds, giving his face an eerie glow. "What the hell?" Decker muttered to himself as he headed for the door keeping the pistol ready. Just because it was a police car out front, didn't mean that it was cops in it. A healthy dose of paranoia had kept him alive back in the day when he had been one of the top undercover operatives for the DEA.

Even though he had retired from the Drug

Enforcement Administration several years ago, he still had a few pissed off dealers that he had busted who tried to look him up. To be on the safe side he had applied for and gotten his private investigator's license and kept his gun permit current. It saved time when he had to shoot one of the assholes.

The knock on his door was certainly loud and official sounding. It sounded again as he reached the picture window. Decker ran his fingers through his light-brown hair, pushing it back and out of his face. He tugged part of the curtain back and looked out. Officer Rufus Drake was standing in front of the door, tapping his foot impatiently as he reached up to rap on the door once more with the butt of his MagLite. Decker felt himself almost grin as he reached over and yanked the door open. Drake stumbled inside.

"What do you want, Rufus?" Decker asked as the young man gained his composure. Rufus Drake weighed about one hundred and sixty-five pounds soaking wet. He was also a bit over six-feet, six-inches tall. With his head shaved bald, he looked like nothing so much as a walking penis, which was probably why he had acquired the nickname "Dickhead" back in high school. It was, however, one that he had never managed to live down.

"Chief wants to see you, Decker," Rufus said, trying to sound official.

"About what?" Decker looked amused, fighting to keep the grin off his face as Drake tried to regain his composure.

"A dead body. Your name was next to it. She told me to come get you and bring you back to the crime scene," Rufus said, almost stumbling over the words.

"Give me a few minutes to get dressed, Rufus. I'll be happy to accompany you," Decker shoved the pistol into the waistband of his shorts. Drake had not even noticed the gun.

"Take your time, just do it quick," Rufus said, his blue eyes wide. Decker shook his head. The kid had a whole lot to learn about police work.

"Make yourself some coffee, Rufus," Decker pointed towards the kitchen. The young cop headed immediately in that direction. Decker watched him go. He would have to talk to Monica Sinclair about the kid.

Monica Sinclair was the local Chief of Police for Scorpion Cay. She was also as tough as nails and balls-to-the-wall former NYPD detective. She had left the New York Police Department to take the job as Chief of the small Scorpion Cay department. Decker knew her socially from karaoke night at the Parrot's Beak. They had danced a few times and he had bought her a few drinks while they told war stories to each other. His of the DEA and hers of the NYPD. He liked and respected her, which was more than he could say for a lot of cops he knew.

Decker got dressed, opting to go ahead and wear his gun in a shoulder holster beneath white tropical weight sports coat. If Sinclair wanted him at a crime scene, there had to be something going on. She disliked private investigators on principle, and he was no exception. He stepped outside; pausing only long enough to turn and make sure his front door was locked. He had made too many enemies over the years to ever be *that* careless!

Drake was sitting in the car, looking impatient and tapping his thumbs nervously on the steering wheel. The plastic coffee mug he had borrowed was sitting on the dash. Decker fought to keep the grin off his face as he deliberately took his time walking around to the passenger side of the vehicle and climbing in. Rufus put the patrol car in reverse and was about to step on the gas.

"Do you really want to wear that coffee?" Decker asked, reaching up and grabbing the mug. Drake's face turned red.

"Sorry, I forgot about that," Drake slowly backed

the car out of the drive and onto the street.

"No problem. It'd be pretty hard explaining to the Chief why your pants were wet though," Decker dumped the coffee out the window as Drake put the car in gear. Decker tossed the plastic mug into his yard. He would pick it up when he got back.

****

Decker was surprised when Rufus pulled up in front of the home of Russell Cosgrove. Cosgrove was a well-known lawyer and one of Scorpion Cay's leading citizens, as well as being an old friend. Cosgrove had been a prosecutor back when he had been working for the DEA. The man had earned his respect back then, and still had it. The fact that his lovely wife had won the Thursday night karaoke competition they had both been entered in meant nothing.

Jessica Monroe had a beautiful voice. Decker had no difficulty in seeing how he had lost to her. Her rendition or "Mercedes Benz" put Janis Joplin to shame! He found himself wondering just where the lady of the house was, and if she was a suspect. He would hate to think so, but a significant other or spouse was *always* the first suspect in a murder case.

Exiting the car, Decker was still wondering why

Monica Sinclair wanted to see him about it. There was no history between the two of them, other than some mutual respect and drinking in at The Parrot's Beak. As he entered the house, Monica was waiting for him.

"Decker, glad to see you could make it," Sinclair looked at him as he entered the living room.

"Like I had a choice," he shook his head.

"You always have a choice. It just depends on the choice you make," Monica replied, her blue eyes meeting his.

"So why did you send Rufus to get me?" Decker scanned the room with his eyes. Nothing appeared out of place.

"How well do you know Russell Cosgrove?" Monica's voice gave nothing away.

"Fairly well, I guess. He prosecuted some of my cases before he left to go into private practice. He was fair and liked things by the book. To the best of my knowledge there wasn't any sort of personal animosity between us," Decker frowned. He was starting to get a bad feeling about where the line of questioning might be headed.

"What about Miss Monroe?" Monica was watching him closely, almost too closely.

"A pretty girl. We compete against each other

regularly in the weekly karaoke contest at the Parrot's Beak. Seems like a nice kid and she's a talented singer too," Decker leveled his gaze to meet hers.

Russell Cosgrove has been murdered," her voice was flat and emotionless as she delivered the news.

"Again I ask, why am I here?" It was out there now, between them. Decker looked at her expectantly.

"Your name and telephone number were on a bloody legal pad next to the body."

"Who found the body?"

"Jessica Monroe. She called 911 in hysterics."

"Walking in on this could certainly cause hysteria."

"Do you have a time of death yet?"

"Maybe. We're waiting on the Medical Examiner to confirm it though."

"Snow's here already?" Decker raised both eyebrows in disbelief.

"I said we're *waiting* on the Medical Examiner," Sinclair half-smiled. Decker couldn't repress a chuckle.

Scorpion Cay Medical Examiner Lucius Snow was the island's only doctor. He was also eighty years old, near-sighted and hard of hearing. Decker almost felt sorry for whichever deputy had been sent to roust the ME from his bed.

"You want me to take a look at the body?" It seemed like a practical question for him to ask.

"You're the only other person on this island with any kind of practical experience in investigating a homicide. My force, God love them, most of them couldn't find their collective asses with both hands and a flashlight!" Sinclair sounded sad as she said it.

"You're wanting my help on this?" Decker couldn't mask his surprise.

'Yeah. You've got a good reputation as a straight shooter, and I talked to Greg Jawolsky over at DEA in Miami. He said you could help me, that you were one of the best investigators that had ever worked for him. Right now, I'm handicapped by a force that the biggest things they have ever dealt with are B and E's and maybe an occasional rape. Most of them are scared shitless that they might trip over a crime. So what would your guess be?" she arched an eyebrow at him.

"Okay I can see your point. I don't work for free though." Decker leaned against the doorway.

"You're already on the books as Scorpion Cay's chief investigator. You're pulling down five hundred bucks a week. Raise your right hand," She ordered. Decker raised his right hand.

"You're officially deputized. Let's go look at the crime scene," Sinclair turned on her heel and headed for the glass sliding doors that opened onto the patio deck.

Decker stepped out onto the patio. So far, most of the available officers from the Scorpion Cay Police Department had stayed in the house, busy searching for anything that might be of interest. The deck was untouched. Decker scanned the wooden planks, noting the splatter pattern of the blood and figured that Cosgrove had been about to get up when he was shot. The bloody legal pad was right next to the folding deck chair, chunks of brain strewn across the yellow paper as well as dried blood. The blood had no doubt soaked into the pad. It was something that Snow would look at in ascertaining the time of death. Decker walked over and squatted next to the body, studying it intently.

"The shot came from over there," Decker stood and pointed to the north corner of the house. Shadows congealed there, creating an even deeper darkness. The perfect place for an assassin to hide.

"That's the way I figure it too. The question is, where did he come from?" Sinclair folded her arms.

"Got a flashlight? We can find out," Decker shrugged out of the white jacket. The dark green shirt he had been wearing underneath blended with the darkness. Decker carried the jacket to the rail and found an area not splattered with blood and gore and laid the jacket across it. Sinclair handed him her MagLite. Decker flicked it on and used the beam to search the sand. It took only seconds to find footprints.

Decker knelt and studied them for a few minutes. The guy had been wearing combat boots with the Panama lug soles. Judging from the depth of the imprint, the killer had weighed over two hundred pounds. Decker flashed the light along the back trail, measuring the length of the man's stride. A six-footer or just slightly taller. He stood and began following the tracks.

Chapter Three

Decker and Sinclair followed the killer's tracks into the night. As they moved farther away from the house, both instinctively drew their pistols. There was no guarantee that the killer wasn't still out there in the darkness of the mangrove trees waiting for them. Both wanted to be ready, just in case.

The tracks led into a stand of mangrove trees about thirty yards from the house. It was easy to see how the killer had been able to approach the exposed deck without being seen by the victim. The sand just inside the tree line was flattened out and a couple of Ziploc bags left behind indicated that the shooter had swum ashore from the ocean.

"Decker," he turned to face Sinclair. A slight breeze had kicked up and was forcing her to brush stray hairs from her face.

"What?" two steps put him at her side. A scrap of black fabric clung to a broken branch. "Got an evidence bag?" Decker knelt next to the branch. The cloth was worn, the dye faded from black to dark gray.

"Here," Sinclair placed a folded small brown paper bag in his right hand. Decker flipped it open and slipped it around the fabric, then nudged the scrap of cloth from the branch so that it fell into the bag, making a soft rustling sound as it hit bottom. Sinclair then gave him a small numbered plastic tag that he affixed to the branch with a twist tie.

"Thanks," Decker stood and handed the bag back to her. Two sets of tracks, one leading from the ocean, the other heading back into the surf. "Well, we know where he came ashore and where he went back into the water. There was obviously a boat out there waiting on the killer."

"So a professional job?" Sinclair dug a pack of cigarettes from her blouse pocket and shook one free and then fired it up.

"Those things will kill ya. Yeah, a professional all the way in my opinion," Decker shrugged. He made it a point to stand upwind of her as she smoked.

"You one of those health nuts that believe all that anti-smoking shit you see on TV?" Sinclair blew a cloud of smoke out.

"Nope. I used to smoke but I quit. Every time I get around it, the craving hits. I just try not to give in," Decker looked out over the moon lit waves. "If the killer is the kind of pro I think he is, then he would have watched the house for several days. Which means, he had to have used the Marina if only to fuel up. If the killer did use the marina, there should be a record of it."

"You want to go check those records?" Sinclair looked at him, puffing on her smoke. Her eyes were black in the moonlight.

"Worth a shot," Decker turned to face her. Her face looked pale in the moonlight, her eyes black and shadowed.

"Go for it. Call me with the results," Sinclair flipped her butt towards the surf, the stub of a cigarette hissing as it made contact with the sea.

"How much latitude are you willing to give me?" Decker focused on her face.

"As much as we need to get the people that did this," Sinclair met his gaze. Decker nodded and started back towards the house. Sinclair followed, just a step or two behind him. A new sound reached their ears. Reflexively Decker drew his pistol again as the distinctive *whup-whup* of helicopter rotary blades became identifiable.

"We have company," Sinclair didn't sound happy. Decker allowed himself a small grin. Russell Cosgrove was well known and respected in the Keys. Once word got out that he had been killed, the Florida Department of Law Enforcement was going to try and get involved. Especially since they had much better facilities than the small Scorpion Cay department. The State police would do all they could to take over and take the glory for solving the case.

"Yeah, probably the FDLE," Decker agreed as they walked out into the open. The helicopter was swinging in low over the house. At least they had the good sense to land in the front and not the rear where the rotor wash could disturb the tracks by blowing sand in them.

"Fuck those assholes. This is *my* case and I'll be damned if they steal it from me." Sinclair started walking faster. Decker grinned. This was a confrontation he wanted to witness!

Mitchell Tanner was at the front door trying to get Rufus Drake to let him into the house. Tanner was one of the top investigators for the Florida Department of

Law Enforcement. Decker knew him by more than just reputation. He had worked with Tanner before and knew him to be a stand-up kind of guy. The man with Tanner however had a far less than sterling reputation. Benito Juarez, a.k.a. Benny the Jet. Juarez was suspected of aiding and abetting more then thirty drug dealers escape arrest. Nothing had ever been proven, but most DEA agents and cops in the Miami area took it as fact. If Benny the Jet was on a case, the perp would vanish before he could ever be picked up.

"Mitch Tanner, as I live and breathe," Decker said as he and Sinclair approached the house.

"Sam Decker? Why are you here?" Tanner looked shocked.

"Working the case for the Scorpion Cay Police Department. What are you and Benny doing here?" Decker regarded both men cynically.

"Russell Cosgrove was an important man. We heard the call, thought maybe y'all could use some help," Tanner replied stiffly.

"Y'all figured us poor local bumpkins couldn't handle a case of such magnitude, did ya?" Sinclair asked sweetly, her voice so sweet it sounded like a marshmallow soaked in honey.

"Something like that, Chica, let us men handle this case. Something this high profile is too big for such a little department" Juarez grinned, showing a mouthful of bright white teeth that contrasted sharply with his darker Hispanic skin.

"No, you listen you little wetback snake! This murder took place in *my* jurisdiction that makes it *my* case! Now haul your Puerto Rican ass the hell out of my crime scene before I cut off your cojones and have them for breakfast," it was said sweetly enough, but Sinclair's New York attitude was coming through loud and clear. Decker couldn't help himself, he started to laugh. A moment later, Tanner was laughing as well.

"You can't do that, lady," Juarez grinned at her.

"Want to bet on it?" Sinclair asked, her voice cold and flat, her eyes giving him her best NYPD stare. "I could arrest your ass for disrupting my crime scene Sonny." Juarez looked over at Tanner.

"Yes, she can if you go in there uninvited," Tanner told him. Juarez glared at her.

"You won't get away with this bitch!"

"Want to bet on that?" Sinclair batted her eyes sweetly.

"Benny unless you want to see the inside of a cell,

back off," Decker inserted himself between the two. Juarez gave him the eye for a long moment and then stepped back. Decker looked over at Tanner. "We'll keep you informed," he said. Tanner nodded his head then took Juarez by the arm and led him back towards the helicopter.

"Thanks," Sinclair said. Decker turned to look at her.

"Don't mention it. Benny Juarez taking such an interest means something. I'm just not sure what," Decker brushed a stray lock of reddish brown hair from his forehead.

"Yeah, that one was *way* too curious. I'll have him put on the watch list," Sinclair looked at him.

"What?" Decker asked.

"You know, Tanner. What's he like?"

"He's a straight shooter. Unlike Juarez who is as crooked as a snake's back," Decker told her truthfully.

"That's what I thought. Go check out the marina and keep me informed," Sinclair ordered.

"Aye aye, Chief," Decker grinned.

*****

Rufus Drake drove him back to his bungalow and dropped him off. Decker watched Drake drive off before walking up to his front door. Drake was something else.

He had peppered Decker with questions all the way back to the house. Rufus had acted almost like a puppy dog yearning for attention. Shaking his head, Decker unlocked his door and stepped inside. If he was going to have to ride his Bike down to the marina, the suit jacket was going to have to go. He was reaching for the light switch when something slammed into the side of his head out of the darkness.

Decker hit the wall seeing stars, felt himself sliding down it as pain exploded in his ribs. He hit the floor, curling up in a fetal position as another kick slammed into his thigh, almost making his leg go totally numb. Whoever was pounding on him was big, Decker knew he needed to even the odds and fast! He rolled, catching the next kick as the booted foot was swinging in on him, grabbing the foot and shoving up and backwards, lifting his attacker in to the air and dropping the guy on his back. As the huge body slammed to the floor, nearly knocking several pictures off the wall, Decked clawed the Sig 228 9mm loose from his shoulder holster. Scrambling to his feet he kicked his attacker hard between the legs, eliciting a loud scream, then he thumbed back the pistol's hammer in a very theatrical move. The click of the hammer locking back was deafening loud in the sudden silence. "Move and I'll blow your fucking head off!" Decker gasped for breath, trying to focus his eyes as they adjusted to the dark.

"Decker? Sam Decker?" rumbled a familiar voice.

"Oso? Is that you?" Decker squinted, but kept the muzzle of his pistol steady.

"What the fuck did Benny get me into? He didn't tell me you were the guy that lived here, Sam," Oso "Bear" Delgado sat up, clutching as his crotch as Decker turned on the light.

"Somebody sent you here?" Decker still kept the pistol pointed at Delgado. Bear Delgado was an old informant he had used during his days as a DEA agent. He hadn't seen much of him since he had quit the agency.

"I just said that, I thought," Delgado groaned.

"Who?"

"Benny the Jet. He called and told me there was five c-notes in it for me if I beat the shit out of the dude that lives here. I figured what the heck I could use the money," Delgado shrugged.

"You almost got a bullet, Bear," Decker wiggled the muzzle of the Sig.

"Yeah, and a pair of sore nuts," Delgado groaned.

"Those you deserved. Now get the fuck out of my house, Oso. And if I *ever* see you near my place without an invitation again, I'll make sure certain people find out you're on the DEA payroll."

"I'm gone, Decker. For what it's worth, I'm sorry. If I knew Benny was sending me after you, I would have turned him down."

"Sure you would, Oso. Now get out of here."

Delgado nodded as he slowly climbed to his feet and staggered for the door. Once the steel lined door had shut behind Delgado, Decker locked the dead bolt. His side and leg and head were all throbbing, part of it due to his lack of sleep as well as the beating he had just taken. Groaning he reholstered his pistol and headed for the bathroom. Two aspirin and a glass of water later, Decker was shrugging into a khaki photographer's vest and heading out the back door. His midnight black Harley Davidson Night Train waited there. The V-twin 1,450 cc engine rumbled to life with a quick kick, then he was pulling out onto the street, heading towards the marina.

Chapter Four

Jessica Monroe couldn't sleep. Every time she closed her eyes, she could still see Russell on the deck, his head surrounded by a pool of blood. Who had killed him and why? She knew he had been working on an important merger for one of his oldest clients. She also knew that he wasn't overly happy with some of the clients that the new partners had brought to his firm. Could that have something to do with why he had been killed? Could it have been the revenge of an old client or enemy that he had once prosecuted? Or did it have anything to do with Russell at all?

Maybe Russ had been killed to throw everyone off. She choked back a sob. Maybe David had found her at last.

He was certainly brutal enough to have done it, leaving Russ there dead for her to find. David was not the kind of man to take her leaving lying down. No, he would have to retaliate, no matter how long it took.

Jessica rolled off the bed and walked to the small built in bar. She removed a bottle of rum and poured herself a tumbler of it. She added enough coca-cola to flavor it, then took a deep drink. Making a face as it burned its way down to her stomach, she added a couple of ice cubes from the bucket of ice and then carried her drink to the balcony. Chief Sinclair had put her up in the best hotel on the island. There was a female police officer stationed outside her door, more to give her peace of mind than any real protection.

Defending her against a killer was way out of the Scorpion Cay department's league. Sure, the Chief was a former NYPD detective, but the rest of the force was strictly small town. Jessica knew that Sinclair was going to want to question her in the morning. The thing was, she had no idea what kind of questions that the woman might ask. Would they be about Russ, his business, or would they be about her, and her past? Drinking deeply she shrugged. There was no way to know.

There was so much of her past that she had tried to

run and hide from. Now, it stood a good chance of catching up with her. Would Sinclair understand why she had changed her name, gone to the lengths that she had gone to in order not to ever be found by anyone from her old life? Would she understand why she had run away from David and the horrors that he had put her through? She drained her glass and walked back to the bed. Setting the empty tumbler on the nightstand, Jessica crawled back into the bed and under the covers. With luck, this time she would be able to go to sleep.

*****

The Marina was quiet as Sam Decker entered the parking lot on his Harley. The bike had a good muffler on it, especially since he didn't always want people to know he was coming. He could hear drums pounding softly in the early morning air. Not party drums, but Voodoo Drums. Mama Celeste was still entertaining. He shrugged it off as he shut down the Harley and strolled down the wooden plank walk to the Marina office. There were no lights on inside, which meant that Joey Fishbine was either not at home, which was very unlikely, or fast asleep. If he was asleep, Decker was about to ruin his night.

Decker kicked the Office door four times, each successively harder until a light clicked on in the back.

Decker felt himself grin as he heard a loud yelp from inside followed by *a lot* of cursing. Seconds later he could see Fishbine limping towards the door.

"What the fuck do you want?" Fishbine growled as he opened the door. Decker shouldered his way through the door, pushing Fishbine back hard as he did so. Decker held up the badge Sinclair had given him.

"Official business. I need to see the log for the last week," Decker crowded forward, not giving the Marina operator time to catch a breath or think.

"When did you become a local cop?" Fishbine asked, his tone nasty as he backed towards the counter.

"Nothing better come up from under that counter but the log book," Decker said pointedly, his hand encircling the butt of his pistol.

"Gee Whiz, Decker! What kind of idiot do you think I am?"

"Joey, how many times you been busted for dealing?"

"Too many."

"Exactly. Considering I got you several times before I left the DEA. I've managed to keep you in the clear since I retired, but only just. One more bust, you could find yourself over on the mainland doing hard time,"

Decker almost whispered.

"You think I don't know that?" Fishbine asked.

"I know you *think* you got connections in Miami and New York, but Joey, *they* can't help you right now," Decker said coldly.

"Yeah, Yeah I get that, Decker. What's so important about the log book for the last week?" Fishbine held out the black leather book where everyone that docked at the Marina had to sign in on.

"Russell Cosgrove was murdered tonight. Whoever did it had to have cased his place from a boat," Decker replied.

"Well shit."

"Exactly." Decker took the log and opened it to the current date. His eyes scanned down the page, dismissing names he recognized and focusing on people not from the island. One name stuck out. He handed the book back to Fishbine. "Make me a copy of the last week of entries."

"No problem Decker. Anything I can do to help, I be happy to do so," Joey said, his voice taking on an island lilt since he now knew he was no longer the focus of any kind of investigation. Decker had a hunch that if he searched the place, he could find a lot of shit that could send Joey up. He had a strong feeling that Joey knew it too.

"It'll take me about five minutes to copy those pages for you, Decker. You want to put some coffee on for me?" Fishbine asked.

"You need a cup of coffee to work the copy machine to copy seven pages out of the log book Joey?" Decker leaned against the counter and started looking the room over closely.

"No but since between you and the drums going non-stop over at Mama Celeste's place, I don't think I'm gonna get a whole lot of sleep tonight," Joey grumbled as he turned the copier on.

"Hey you seemed to be doing fine until I knocked on your door," Decker started across the room toward a file cabinet. Fishbine had been shooting nervous glances towards it the entire time he had been inside the office.

"Where you going, Decker?"

"Just having a look around, Joey," Decker yanked open the file cabinet drawer. Four bags of pot were stuffed in there atop the files. Decker turned to look at Joey Fishbine who was now *very* pale.

"I never saw it before in my life," Joey said as he ran the first copy of the log.

"You telling me this shit just bagged itself and

walked in on its own and climbed into your filing cabinet?"
Decker grinned.

"Shit!"

"Exactly," Decker said, picking up the three zip-
lock bags and carrying them into the office bathroom. He
opened the bags and dumped the contents into the toilet
then flushed it. The bags he kept, knowing that he had Joey
by the balls since his prints were all over them. "You know
what this is?" Decker held up the bags, now almost empty.

"What?" Joey asked resignedly.

"Trace evidence. I got enough here to send your ass
to the mainland for about *twenty years* given your record.
Do not *fuck* with me in *any* way shape or form, Joey. You
hear *anything*, you call me first!" Decker told him, stuffing
the bags into the pockets of his vest.

"Like I got a choice," Joey said, hanging his head.
He took a sheaf of papers from the tray below the copier
and handed them to Decker.

"Thanks for your cooperation, Joey. Remember,
anything comes to mind, call me," Decker said, turning on
his heel and walking out the door, letting the outer screen
door bang shut behind him.

The drums were much louder outside. Decker
looked over towards Mama Celeste's house and then turned

and headed that direction. He had never known her to be conducting rituals this late.

The drums were coming through loud-speakers aimed out towards the bay. Decker started to knock on the door and then noticed it was partially open. Instinctively his hand found the butt of his pistol and drew it from the holster beneath his vest. His thumb found the safety and released it, getting the Sig ready to fire. Using his foot he nudged the door open. The drums were almost deafening inside the small shack.

The smell hit him before anything else. Hot and coppery, the scent of blood was thick in the air. Death had come to visit at Mama Celeste's house. Decker stepped to the side so he wasn't backlit by the lights of the Marina parking lot. He took a few moments, letting his eyes adjust to the darkness inside the house.

Monica Sinclair was not going to be happy. One murder on the island was news. Two was an epidemic. He felt himself grimace. There might not be a way to keep the FDLE out of things now. He didn't like the idea of Benny The Jet getting too close to any part of the investigations, but it might happen. Monica might have no choice

Decker spotted a switch plate on the wall and reached over, using the muzzle of his pistol to flip the light on. To Decker's surprise, the body bleeding out on the floor was not Mama Celeste. It was a white male, approximately six feet tall, and around two hundred pounds, at least more or less when alive.

Chapter Five

Decker pulled out his flip phone and dialed Monica Sinclair. She answered on the second ring. "Chief Sinclair."

"I've got the logs but I've got bad news as well," Decker scanned the scene with his eyes. He wanted to see what he could see.

"Seems like that's all I'm getting tonight,' Monica sighed.

"There's been another murder. At least I have a dead body on the floor of Mama Celeste's place and our local voodoo priestess is nowhere to be found," Decker knelt down, getting a different perspective on the scene.

"Shit! Snow isn't even finished with this body yet, and now you have another one for him?" he could hear the weariness in her voice.

"Two murders in one night, it might be harder to keep FDLE out of it," Decker noticed something lying just under the body.

"I know, but dammit we're going to do our best. I'll send somebody over to help you secure the scene. I hate the idea that somebody thinks they can get away with this shit on my watch," Monica sighed.

"I know. I may have something here. Yeah, I do. It's a business card," Decker eased the card from beneath the body.

"Who does it belong to?" Monica's voice seemed to catch over the connection.

"Russell Cosgrove," Decker read the name aloud. Both of the murders looked to be connected. Decker climbed to his feet. "I'm getting a bad feeling about this."

"You and me both. I'm coming over personally, Sam."

"I kinda figured you would, Monica. Right now I'm going to find the stereo system and shut down the drums. Damn things are giving me a headache," Decker broke the connection and flipped the phone shut.

Decker moved carefully around the body and found the switch to the stereo system. It was a relief when the pounding of the drums stopped, yet the air held an eerie silence now. He felt a chill race down his spine as he turned. A thin black woman stood there, her lined face impassive as her dark eyes watched him. "Mama Celeste, I've been looking for you," Decker said, trying to regain his composure.

"I know dat, Sammy Boy. I left earlier because the

loa told me dat de Baron he be coming to call tonight. I see dat he done been and gone," Mama Celeste said.

"How did you know I'd be here?" Decker asked, more than a little surprised.

"You come about de boat and about dat lawyer man dat was killed on de other side o' de island. The loa spoke to me, told me I needed to prepare a gris-gris for you. One to keep you safe. Dark forces coming to play on de island, Sammy Boy. You best be careful," she smiled, showing him some missing teeth.

"I'm a real careful guy, Mama. You know who this man on the floor might be?" Decker wanted to turn the body over but knew better than to disturb it before crime scene photos were taken.

"He been askin' around about dat lawyer man dat got killed earlier tonight. He talked to Joey earlier," Mama shrugged. Decker thought about that for a moment. He'd pay Joey another visit after Monica arrived to take charge of the crime scene. The little weasel had been less than forth-coming tonight. He could and should have mentioned the man when Decker was copying the log.

Jessica Monroe threw the covers off and rolled to her feet. Even with the patio doors open and the breeze blowing the curtains, the room felt oppressively hot. Jessica walked to the balcony and stepped out on it past the billowing white curtains. The moon was lower in the sky and she could see the first pink tendrils of light creeping over the horizon. The quiet was the first thing she noticed. The drumbeat that had been audible all over the island had stopped.

Closing her eyes, she saw Russell as he had looked just before she had left to go to The Parrot's Beak. Hot tears spilled from her eyes, burning their way down her cheeks. Jessica gripped the balcony railing tighter, feeling the metal cut into her palms. She had to know why Russell had died. There was one man on the island that might be able to find out. Sam Decker. He had used to work for the Drug Enforcement Agency, but since retiring from the DEA he had gone to work as a Private Investigator. She'd hire him. From what she knew about him from competing in the weekly karaoke contest, he certainly seemed capable enough. Maybe more than the local cops.

Wiping her eyes, Jessica turned and stepped back into her room. Just then the glass doors of the patio exploded into shards. Jessica dived to the floor and crawled for cover as the sound of the first shot echoed into the room. The bedside lamp exploded under the impact of another bullet, drawing another scream from her. She could hear the policewoman pounding on the door, demanding to know what was happening and if she was okay. Jessica snatched her laptop from the nightstand, cutting her hand in the process. Another bullet thwacked into the wall above her head. Then the silence returned.

The door to the room flew open and the policewoman stood in the doorway, her gun drawn. "Miss Monroe? Are you okay?" the cop shouted, stepping inside, trying to cover the whole room with her service weapon.

"I'm bleeding," Jessica called back, sitting up.

"Wrap something around it and crawl over here. We need to get you out of here," the cop said, never taking her eyes off the remains of the patio doors.

"I can do that. Do you think whoever was shooting is still out there?" Jessica asked, fear making her voice quiver.

"I don't know," the woman replied.

"Okay, I'm crawling over. Do you have a name?" Jessica asked. It helped her to have something to focus on. Knowing the cop's name would give her a focal point.

"Nora Santiago. You were too upset earlier to remember when I told you," the cop replied.

"Sorry about that, Nora. I was upset about my

husband then," Jessica said, trying to be gracious under pressure.

"Not a problem. I was the same way when my father died. My husband talked to me for about an hour and I went to sleep and remembered nothing about the conversation at all," Nora Santiago replied, holstering her pistol and reaching out. Jessica took her hand and Santiago pulled her forward out of the line of fire.

Monica Sinclair was halfway to the Marina when she heard the three loud booms rolling across the island like thunder. Monica recognized the report of a high-powered rifle. She immediately reached for the radio even before she heard Nora Santiago calling in the shot's fired at the hotel.

Monica threw her police car into a tight turn and headed for the hotel, letting Santiago know she was on the way. Rufus, God help them, had also responded that he was on the way as well.

Monica chewed her bottom lip as she drove. The job down here in the keys was supposed to be nice and quiet, a break from all of the high-crime and violence of New York City. Fat chance of that! Now at least two if not three murders in one night?

Not to mention the fact that she had both state and federal boys wanting to come in and ride roughshod over her jurisdiction because of the political ramifications of the first murder. Monica shook her head. At least Decker had been willing to come on board long enough help work the case.

She liked the retired DEA agent. He was sharp and funny as well as being reasonably attractive for an old guy. She felt the corner of her mouth twitch up in a smile. At thirty-four she wasn't exactly a spring chicken herself. Not that she was old or anything, far from it. But the older she got, the more limited her options were, both romance and career-wise.

Monica was out of her car almost before it had stopped and was running for the door of the hotel. She hoped that Jessica Monroe wasn't hurt, but there was no way to know that yet. Whoever was trying to kill the young woman, for whatever reason, was certainly determined. Was this attack because they had missed when her boyfriend had been executed last night? Or was it something else entirely? Monica opened the door and stepped inside.

Nora Santiago was just stepping off the elevator, her service pistol in hand, Jessica Monroe behind her. Monroe had a blood-soaked cloth wrapped around one hand and was clutching a laptop computer to her chest. "Was she hit?" Monica asked.

"No, just a cut from a shard of broken glass," Nora replied, eyes scanning everything. Monica couldn't help smiling. Nora was one of her best officers and the mostly likely to become an investigator. She had the instincts.

"How do you think they found her?" Monica asked.

"Only two hotels on the island. I'd say that they probably checked them out to see if we had a room booked," Nora shrugged.

"Where can we put her?" Monica asked, not sure what to do next.

"I'll take her home with me," Nora said.

Rufus Drake came running into the lobby of the hotel, his gun drawn and ready for action. "Holster that, Rufus," Monica ordered. Drake obeyed, looking dumb-founded. It was obvious from his expression he had hoped to be a hero when he arrived. Getting there and finding everything was under control was obviously a let-down.

"What happened?" Rufus asked.

"Somebody found our witness. I want you to go up to her room and secure it until we can get some people up there to process it. I mean it Rufus, nobody goes in or out until I say different," Monica ordered.

"Yes, Ma'am!" Rufus snapped a saluted and headed for the elevator. Monica turned to see Nora smiling at her.

"What?" she asked.

"You did good making him feel important," Nora smiled.

"It got him out of the way," Monica shrugged. "How bad is that cut?" Jessica looked over at her.

"It might need stitches," Jessica said

"Swing by Doc Halloran's place and get it looked at, then take her home. You think she'll survive the kids?" Monica grinned.

"She'll do just fine," Nora replied. With that, they walked her out to Nora's car. Monica watched them drive away and then went back inside. She wanted a look at the room herself. Her cell phone vibrated in her pocket and she pulled it out. It was Decker. Crap, she had forgotten all about him. Monica flipped the phone open.

"Sinclair," she said.

"What's been happening, Monica? I heard the shots," Decker's voice sounded in her ear.

"Somebody took some shots at Miss Monroe. I'm having her moved," Monica pressed the button for the fifth floor. That was the one that Monroe's room had been on.

"Why were they shooting at her?" Decker asked.

"That's the question. Anyway did Tom and Gina get there yet?" Monica watched the numbers pass by as the elevator rose.

"Yeah, they're taking photos and working the scene now. Mama Celeste turned up, said this guy had been asking a lot of questions about Cosgrove. I'm going to walk back over and ask Joey why he left that information out," Decker told her.

"Do it. If that weasel is holding out information I'll see his butt in the state pen before the sun sets," Monica stepped out of the elevators. "I'll talk to you later."

Sam Decker snapped his phone closed, smiled at Mama Celeste, and then started back across the parking lot. The sun was just starting to come up over the ocean in what was looking to be a beautiful Caribbean day. Joey Fishbine was just opening the doors to the Marina office when Decker slammed a fist across his jaw and sent him tumbling back inside.

Fishbine was on the floor rubbing his jaw as Decker stepped inside and shut the door behind him. "What did ya do that for?" Joey asked, looking up at him. Decker felt himself smile as he looked down.

"Joey, we need to talk," Decker said.

Chapter Six

Sam Decker left the Marina and climbed aboard his Harley and kicked it to life. The sun was up but he wanted a few hours of sleep before heading across to Miami to look up the name on the Marina log. He was pretty sure it would lead nowhere, but he needed to check it out. It was a name from the past.

*****

Mac Donnelly wiped the sweat from his brow as they crouched in the jungle together. Decker took a drink from his canteen, grateful for the moisture. "How long?" he asked. Donnelly shrugged his wide shoulders.

"Not much longer. Cruz and Alvarado like to stay on schedule," Donnelly replied.

"You're sure this is the place they always meet?" Decker was getting anxious.

"They'll be here. Hell, Sam, I helped set this place up while working under cover," Donnelly swatted at a mosquito. Just then the soft rumble of a boat engine became audible. Both of them hunkered down in the vegetation sweating palms gripping their weapons. Decker watched as two boats motored into the small cove and the engines idled. He recognized both of them. Eduardo Cruz and Maximillian Alvarado. One represented the cartels, the other a major distributor for cocaine in south Florida. There were a total of three two man teams spread around the cove for this bust. Baker and Flores were right across from them, and Sims and Juarez were near the entrance.

Decker frowned as he thought of Benito Juarez. Benny the Jet as he was known on the street. It was starting to seem like a lot of the big fish were starting to slip through the net when Juarez was involved on a case. He hoped that this wasn't one of those cases.

"Ready, Sam?" Mac whispered from beside him. Decker felt himself nod.

"Let's do it." Then he was up, leveling his M-16 and yelling, "DEA stop right there!" Cruz spun towards them, pistol in hand. Decker squeezed the trigger and felt the M-16 rattle in his fists. Cruz tumbled backwards off his boat into the water. Donnelly was running towards the

dock and out over the water. Baker and Flores were doing the same. More gunfire erupted and Decker watched in horror as Mac Donnelly tumbled off the dock and into the water. A second later Cruz' boat exploded in a brilliant flash of white."

*****

Decker awoke in a cold sweat, the sheets of his bed soaked. He glanced at the clock next to the bed, surprised to see it was early afternoon. He hadn't thought about Mac Donnelly in years. Not until he had seen that name in the Marina log book. To the best of his knowledge, Mac had died that day in the cove. And though he couldn't prove it was Benny the Jet that had pulled the trigger, in his gut he knew it was true.

George Sims had caught a stray round and died that day as well. The only survivors had been Decker and Juarez. Alvarado had gotten away clean. That had been the start of why he didn't like Benito Juarez. There had been other reasons that had built up over the years.

Decker put on coffee and by the time he had finished his shower it was done. He poured a cup and drank it as he dressed. Since he was representing the Scorpion Cay Police Department, he felt like he should dress the part. Decker chose a pair of khaki cargo pants and a light blue long sleeved shirt, black tie and khaki blazer. The blazer he left unbuttoned to make the pistol on his hip less conspicuous. This trip he would be taking his vintage 1965 forest green Ford Mustang, especially since he was going to pay a call on a man who might be able to give him some answers about what Russell Cosgrove had uncovered that might have gotten him killed.

First, however, Decker planned to call on Jessica Monroe and see what light she might be able to shed on Cosgrove's murder. Carrying his mug of coffee with him, Decker stepped outside. He was more than a little surprised to see Mitch Tanner sitting in a rented Ford Escort outside in the driveway.

Decker walked over to the car and looked in at him. Sweat was beaded on his forehead. "To what do I owe this honor, Mitch?" Decker grinned.

"How about getting in here so I can turn on the air-conditioning? It's hotter than hell out here," he replied.

"Been waiting long?" Decker asked, checking out the wet patches on his shirt where sweat had soaked the material.

"Get in the fucking car already," Mitch growled. Grinning Decker walked around to the passenger side and got in. He immediately turned the engine on and cranked the air-conditioning up to full blast. He left his window down for a few minutes to blow some of the hot air out before rolling it up. The air inside the car began to cool rapidly. Decker looked at him expectantly as the silence hung thickly in the air between them. Mitch shifted uncomfortably in his seat as Decker watched, finally Decker broke the silence and let him off the hook.

"Well?" Decker asked.

"For a woman, that Chief of Police has balls of pure brass," he growled. Decker laughed at him.

"She's from New York, what did you expect? A Southern Belle you could waltz in here and bully into letting you have your way?" Decker sipped at his coffee.

"That would have been nicer," Tanner replied with a grin.

"So Mitch, why exactly is the Treasury Department looking at Russell Cosgrove for?" Decker sipped more of his coffee.

"Actually it wasn't Cosgrove we were looking at. He just happened to come up," Tanner replied.

"Just happened to come up? In such a way that the United States Treasury Department got involved? I don't think so," Decker shook his head.

"You ever hear of a guy named Jerry Contras?" Tanner asked.

"Sure, he's a pretty well-known businessman in Little Havana. Known to contribute to a lot of the Cuba Libra Groups and several charities. Even rumored to have some political ambitions that have the political machine in Miami proper worried," Decker replied, wondering what Jerry Contras had to do with Russell Cosgrove and the Treasury Department.

"Well Cosgrove was handling a merger for Jerry Contras and his Contras Enterprises. It seems Contras was merging with Delacorte Enterprises. Delacorte is owned and run by Miguel Delacorte," Tanner shrugged. Decker thought about that for a long moment.

Miguel Delacorte was bad news. It was rumored that he was moving a lot of product for the Cali Cartel but nothing had ever been proven. He was a Mutt Decker had looked at back during his DEA days. Delacorte was slick enough that Decker could never prove he was into anything, but the gut had said he was dirty as sin.

"So why is Jerry Contras throwing in with Miguel Delacorte?" Decker asked.

"That is a very good question. One we were hoping that Russell Cosgrove could answer," Tanner said.

"And Russell Cosgrove ended up dead before you could ask him," Decker finished his coffee. It wasn't a question.

"Exactly," Tanner affirmed.

"And since Cosgrove was handling the merger between the two companies, he was privy to an inside look at how Delacorte operated," Decker said, following the cop logic.

"Yes," Tanner confirmed. "At least that is what the boys at Treasury think."

"Did Benny the Jet know you were wanting to talk to Cosgrove?" Decker asked, letting it hang in the air between them.

"Yes. Benny was my second on the case," Tanner replied soberly. Decker could tell it upset the hell out of him to admit it by the way his face got redder at the mention of Benny's name.

"You think Benny may have tipped off Delacorte about Treasury's interest in the merger?" Decker asked, putting into words something that Tanner may not have yet been able to say.

"The possibility is there," Tanner admitted. Decker studied his face as he said it. Tanner didn't want to admit his partner was dirty as toilet paper in an outhouse catch basin, but he couldn't afford to ignore the possibility. Especially given Benny's reputation. Decker knew where he was coming from and Tanner knew it too. Decker had gone through his own share of partners while in the DEA and some of them had been rotten to the core.

"I can see how that might be a concern. Especially given Benny's rep for shedding shit every time it hits the fan close to him. So what do you want from me?" Decker asked. He was pretty sure he knew.

"I want you to look into the merger, ask questions, annoy people, do what you do best," Tanner grinned.

"What if I told you that Benny sent a local leg breaker over here last night to try and discourage my involvement in the matter of Russell Cosgrove?" Decker asked.

"Well shit," Mitch said, drawing a pack of cigarettes out of his left shirt pocket and shaking one free. He stuck it in his mouth as he replaced the pack in his pocket and fished for a lighter with his other hand. A moment later he had the smoke lit and was puffing away like a runaway locomotive. Well shit indeed. Shit spelled with a capitol S. Decker looked at Tanner.

"Can you think of a good reason why Benny would do such a thing?" Decker asked.

"Nope. Not one good reason, but lots of bad ones," Tanner replied thoughtfully.

"How much interference can you run between me and Benny?" Decker asked.

"A lot. I'm the primary on this," Tanner replied.

"I may call on you then," Decker said.

"So you'll help me out here?" Tanner asked.

"Yeah. Because it smells worse than a three day old halibut," Decker replied.

"Happy hunting then," Tanner said. Decker accepted the dismissal and climbed out of the car.

"You got Benny for a partner on this one, Mitch, watch your own back," Decker said.

"I will," he replied as Decker shut the door of the car. Mitch Tanner put it in gear and got the hell out of there leaving Decker standing in his drive and wondering what kind of deal he had just gotten himself into. Decker stood and watched him go, and then took his empty coffee mug back into his house. Moments later he was in the mustang with the windows rolled down and driving away.

A quick call to Monica had given him Jessica's whereabouts. Decker knew where Nora Santiago lived since he was a good friend of her husband, Diego. Diego worked hard as a fisherman, and between what he made and what Nora made working for the police department, they did pretty well despite having six kids. The children ranged from a two year old to a seventeen year old. The two older daughters watched the kids when Nora and Diego were working. Decker caught himself grinning, wondering how Jessica was getting along with the kids.

A few minutes later he was braking the Mustang to a stop in front of the Santiago house. It was another small ranch style bungalow. An assortment of children's toys littered the front yard like a non-lethal minefield. Decker put the Mustang in park and shut it off. Then he took a deep breath to prepare himself for the coming ordeal. His resolve readied, Decker climbed out of the Mustang and made his way to the front door.

From inside he could hear the children's voices, chattering away. Decker felt himself smile. Decker had thought about having a family once, but then decided against it. Family made you vulnerable. If you loved something, it gave your enemies and edge because they would know where they could strike at you. For Nora, it was different. Her family grounded her, gave her a purpose for doing The Job. For Decker, family was a risk he was afraid to take.

The door opened and a cute little girl with long black hair and wide, dark brown eyes stood there. She looked to barely be old enough to walk, and he guessed she was probably the four year old. "Yes?" she asked in a very proper and grown up voice.

"My name is Sam Decker. I need to speak to your mother," he told her, flashing his most winning smile.

"One moment, if you please," she replied and the door closed again. In less than a minute, Nora was opening the door, smiling at him.

"The Chief said you would probably be by this morning," she said.

"So nice to know that I'm so predictable," Decker replied as she opened the door and let him inside.

"Only to certain people, Amigo. The young lady you want to see is in the kitchen eating breakfast with the kids."

"Really? And she's still sane?" Decker grinned. Nora was a very pretty woman herself, and if she had been single and without the kids, Decker might have made a run on her himself. Still, they did enjoy a harmless, yet flirtatious relationship.

"Yes, believe it or not, she actually *likes* children."

"Amazing," Decker kidded as he followed her to the kitchen.

"Isn't it though?" Nora asked, looking over her shoulder and batting her eyelashes at him.

Chapter Seven

Jessica Monroe was one of those women who looked fantastic even scared to death and devoid of make-up. She had a flawless complexion that would make a cover girl jealous. Her mane of blonde hair was in disarray from sleep, yet Decker could tell she would still stop traffic if she stepped outside.

"Feeling better today?" Decker asked her as he took a seat at the table. Almost as if by magic, Nora made a plate of eggs and bacon and a cup of coffee appear in front of him. He glanced at her.

"Starving private investigators need to eat too," she said with a grin.

"Yes, Mr. Decker, I am. I want to apologize for my

rude behavior last night," Jessica said. Her voice was soft and low, almost melodic when she spoke. Listening to her talk, he could understand why she was such an excellent singer.

"You won the contest fair and square. If anybody should be apologizing, it's me. I had a bit too much to drink myself," Decker took a bite of his eggs.

"You know about what happened afterwards?" she asked, fear edging her voice.

"Yeah, I heard about your boyfriend, and what happened at the hotel afterwards," Decker nodded, eating more of his bacon and eggs.

"I want to hire you to find out who killed Russell and why," Jessica Monroe looked at him over the top of her coffee mug.

"The police have already hired me to do that," Decker put his fork on the table.

"I know, Chief Sinclair told me that. I need to know why Russell was murdered. I need to know if it was because of something he was doing or because of me," tears were starting to run down her cheeks. Decker sighed. He hated it when they started to cry. Women just didn't play fair.

"Why do you think he was killed because of you?"

He decided to press her on the revelation. Nora appeared as if by magic and handed Jessica a tissue. Decker found himself wondering if the two women had rehearsed the whole scene. Nora looked at him.

"No, Sam, we didn't," she said before turning and leaving the room. He felt himself grin as he refocused his attention back on Jessica Monroe.

"I came to the keys to escape from my past, Mister Decker. Like many others before me," Jessica said.

"True enough," Decker nodded.

"I grew up in the Midwest, Mr. Decker. As soon as I turned eighteen I ran away to New York City. I was young and naive and fell in with some bad people. It took me a long time to get away from them and I came here to start over. I met Russell and he opened up a whole new world for me, a new life. I want to know if my past has caught up with me. And if it has, if Russell paid the price for it," Jessica said, her voice catching.

"I'll keep that in mind, Miss Monroe," Decker nodded.

"Jessica, please. Miss Monroe, well, that name just doesn't even seem real anymore," she shook her head.

"Okay Jessica. Tell me about Russell. What was he working on? Had he mentioned anything?" Decker leaned forward across the table.

"He was working on a merger for one of his oldest clients, a Jerry Contras," she replied.

"Was anything bothering him?" Decker asked, savoring the egg and bacon that Nora had prepared. The coffee was excellent also.

"Something was, Russ was awfully tired. I thought maybe that the new partners weren't carrying their weight, but now I think maybe it had to do something with the merger."

"Such as?" Decker took another sip of coffee.

"I don't know. Russ was edgy. Something wasn't right, but he wasn't prepared to tell Mr. Contras yet," she replied. Her face was open an honest. Decker believed her.

"Do you want me to look into it?" he asked, taking another bite and chewing it.

"I want to know who killed my fiancé and why," she replied, her gaze level with his.

"Even if it might lead to some public embarrassment?" Decker asked.

"No matter where or what it might lead to," she said. He could tell that she meant every word. Decker shrugged and ate some more.

"Good enough," Decker nodded. He had finished

all the food on his plate. "I'll get a contract drawn up and bring it over for you to sign later today."

"What am I paying?" she asked. The woman was much more composed than she had been at The Parrot's Beak.

"A hundred and fifty a day plus expenses," Decker said.

"That sounds reasonable. Can I trust you, Mr. Decker?" she asked. He looked into her eyes.

"Yes," Decker said. He meant it.

"I'll have a thousand dollar retainer ready for you when you bring the contract," she replied soberly. Decker nodded, knowing she was still going to have to undergo a long interview with Brenda.

"I'll do my best for you," Decker told her.

"I know you will," she said with a slight nod of her head.

"Give me authorization in writing to go through Mr. Cosgrove's files. I'll need it," Decker told her. Nora produced a pen and paper. Jessica quickly wrote a note stating that he was to be given full cooperation from the staff at Cosgrove, Martin, and Wilkes. Decker read over it, had Nora sign it as a witness.

"Thanks," Decker looked into her bright blue eyes.

" This will help."

"I want his killer found," she replied. Decker took the paper and headed for the door. He knew Nora would keep a close eye on her, and the kids were a better early warning defense system than NORAD.

A second police car was sitting in front of the house when Decker stepped outside. Monica was sitting there waiting on him. He could tell she wanted to talk since she was standing outside the car, leaning on the front fender. "Monica," he said in greeting.

"Decker. Why did I have to hear from Mitch Tanner you got attacked last night?"

"Mitch has a big mouth. Besides, I took care of it."

"I'm not liking this sudden crime spree that has hit the island," Monica shook her head.

"I'm not fond of it either. Find out anything more about who was shooting at her at the hotel?" Decker brushed a stray lock of hair from his forehead.

"No. We can't even figure for certain where the shots were fired from. Find out anything useful from her?" Monica asked.

"I don't know yet. Maybe," Decker shrugged.

"Got any leads yet?"

"Maybe. I'm heading over to the mainland to talk

to Jerry Contras. Cosgrove was handling a merger for him. According to Miss Monroe, that was the only thing Cosgrove was involved in right now," Decker said.

"Going by yourself?"

"No. I'm taking Rafael Cortez with me."

"Are you nuts? For all you know Cortez might have been the triggerman who took Cosgrove out," Monica said, pushing off the fender of her car.

"So I'll ask him. If he says he didn't, I know he didn't," Decker shrugged, feeling slightly defensive.

"You mean you'd believe him?" she asked, her expression incredulous.

"In a word, yes."

"Quill are you fucking stupid?" she demanded, her voice raising slightly. He looked at her.

"I don't know, am I?" Shaking his head he climbed into the Mustang and fired the engine then drove off, leaving her standing there. As much as he found himself liking the woman, she did have a knack for getting under his skin.

Rafael Cortez was an honorable man. They had known each other when Decker worked for the DEA and Cortez had been an enforcer for a Cuban dealer named Cordova. When Cordova had actually started selling his product to children and trying to entice girls barely in their teens into his bed, Cortez contacted Decker. Cordova had crossed a line in Cortez's mind, relieving him of any obligation he had to the man through his dishonorable actions. After that, Cortez became a private contractor, taking jobs for those who could meet his price as long as the job was one that he could do and still live within his own personal code of honor. Decker had heard through the grapevine that he had even taken a few jobs for the Company; as the spooks at Langley are known to the local Latin American community. An old partner at DEA had confided in Decker that they had hired him a couple of times as well.

Rafael and Decker had developed an uneasy friendship based on their own personal codes. They both knew each other as men who would keep their words. Decker had used him for back up on other occasions when it looked like things could get hairy. Circumstances had proven he had made a wise choice.

Decker figured if anyone might have heard anything going on as far as Russell Cosgrove was concerned, at least on the wrong side of the street, Rafael would know about it, or would know someone who would.

One thing Decker had always noticed about Rafael

Cortez is the stillness that permeated everything around him. It didn't matter if he was sitting by himself in a room with no one else in it, or if he was in the middle of a crowd. There is a space around him that was completely and totally still, nothing moves in it, nothing intrudes into it. Not unless Rafael lets it, which he rarely does.

He was sitting quietly in a back booth of a small bodega in Little Havana, drinking a cup of coffee as he read the newspaper. Rafael is a big guy, but his build is so symmetrical, most people don't realize how big he is until they are standing right next to him. His thick curly hair was slicked back from his forehead, but a few unruly curls had sprung forward and dangled over it. His brown eyes watched Decker as he walked towards the table, and Sam could feel the questions in their gaze. He scooted out a chair at the side of the table and dropped into it, positioning himself where he could see the doorway as well as Rafael. Decker knew he could trust *him*, however he didn't know whom Cortez might have pissed off that might come in looking for him.

"Sam Decker, whatever brings you to visit, Amigo?" he asked, his voice a rich baritone with only a trace of his native Cuban accent. He reminded Decker a lot of Antonio Banderas.

"I was wondering if you were busy this week, Rafe. I'm on a case and I may need some back up," Decker said.

"You?" the amusement was evident through the twinkle in his eyes.

"Even I have my off days. You hear about what happened on the island?"

"It made the morning news. Didn't know you were involved."

"Monica invited me in on it, and Mitch Tanner from the FDLE has given me some unofficial support as well."

"Meaning they want you to solve the case and then they take the credit," he smiled.

"Something like that."

"So what you need me for?"

"Benny the Jet sent some muscle to my house last night, told the guy I was messing around in his business. I know you and Benny are close, thought you might like the opportunity to say hello if he shows up while I'm snooping around," Decker shrugged. A waitress appeared and placed a cup of coffee in front of him. Then she vanished as magically as she had appeared.

"Benny the Jet. You do like to make friends don't you? Okay, Decker, I'm in. Where are we going?"

"You heard of a guy named Jerry Contras?"

"Of course," Cortez replied, looking at him like Decker was wearing a sign that said "stupid" on his forehead.

"You know he was getting ready to merge his company with another one?"

"There's been some talk. Most folks are upset about it; seem to think he's making a big mistake."

"What do you think about it?"

"I don't," Cortez replied with a flash of brilliant white teeth that contrasted sharply with his dark skin.

"And what do you think of Delacorte?"

Cortez shrugged. Decker could take that any number of ways. Decker looked at Cortez with the question evident on his face. "What?" Cortez asked finally.

"You know something about Delacorte," Decker said. It wasn't a question.

"Maybe. I'll go with you, watch your back while you ask your questions. Then, we'll see," Rafe replied soberly.

"Oh boy. You really know how to encourage a person," Decker groused.

"I do my best, Amigo. Let's go for your little drive," Cortez replied with a smile as he stood up. Decker knew that was the best he would get from him at this point.

Decker followed him out the door.

Chapter Eight

It took them about twenty minutes to reach the building that housed Delacorte Enterprises. Together they climbed out of Rafe's car, the noontime sun beating down on them. The building was one of the post modern glass effigies that had sprung up all over Little Havana. It had very little of the neon-art deco architecture that had sprung up all over Miami over the last twenty years. Rafe was behind me as we walked through the plate glass doors.

The reception area in the library was ultra-modern, done up in chrome and glass. A young Hispanic woman, probably Cuban or Guatemalan, sat behind the big chrome-plated reception desk. She was dressed in a black suit with light gray pin-stripes and a short skirt that revealed a lot of nicely tanned leg.

"May I help you?" she asked, smiling at Decker, but

really turning up the wattage on the smile when she spotted Rafael.

"Samuel Decker and associate to see Mr. Delacorte," he smiled back. She looked at Decker like an insect, still trying to concentrate her attention on Rafael.

"Do you have an appointment?" she asked. Decker looked at the nameplate on the desk.

"Rosita, I'm here on behalf of the Scorpion Cay police Department. I want to ask Mr. Delacorte a few questions. Either he agrees to see me, or I get on the radio and have two or three SWAT teams in here busting up all this nice expensive furniture and disturbing the neighbors. I don't think Mr. Delacorte would like that, do you?" Decker asked.

"Probably not," she replied, reaching for the telephone.

"Let him know we're on the way up," Decker said, walking past her towards the elevator.

"I will, Senior," she replied. The elevator doors opened immediately and Rafael and Decker stepped inside. He hit the button-marked penthouse, knowing that was where they would find Miguel Delacorte.

Delacorte had a reputation for trouble, so Cortez and Decker were both ready with pistols drawn when the

elevator stopped at the penthouse and the door opened.
They stepped out of the elevator with pistols drawn, tense
and waiting for any sort of greeting. Neither of them was
prepared for the topless red head that stood there. She wore
nothing but a long mane of heavily layered hair and a string
bikini bottom. Green eyes flashed as she looked them over.

"Mr. Delacorte is expecting you," she told
us. Decker nodded and followed, pistol in hand. The
Penthouse befitted a man of Miguel Delacorte's position
in the community, at least the money end of it. Most scum
sucking drug dealers have lots of cash to throw around,
and Delacorte had blown a wad on the Penthouse. But it
still didn't change what he was, a no-account drug dealer
and smuggler that peddled poison to anybody he could talk
into buying it. Sure, he was accepted as a man of money
in the community, but no one wanted to associate with him
beyond the public dinners and such. Like the lobby, the
furniture in the penthouse was largely chrome steel and
glass.

Miguel Delacorte wasn't a large man, yet he gave
the impression of power. His dark black hair was close
cropped, no doubt to try and mask the fact that his hair was
thinning. His eyes were brown and smoldered with barely
checked rage. Thick gold chains hung around his neck. He

was smoking a fat cigar. His white silk shirt was open to the waist and tucked neatly into the waistband of a pair of khaki Dockers. A shiny Rolex watch adorned his left wrist.

"You don't needs guns to talk to me," Delacorte said, his voice rich and full, but thick with his Cuban accent.

"Funny, that's not what I heard," Decker grinned. "In fact, I heard the only way to talk to you and get answers was with a gun in hand."

"Perhaps I should call the police," Delacorte deadpanned.

"Perhaps you should. Benny the Jet working this part of Miami these days?" Decker shrugged.

"Cortez, why you backing-up this crazy Gringo? You forget where you from? Where you started?" Delacorte addressed Rafael for the first time. Decker held his breath waiting for the answer and not sure what it was going to be.

"I'm here because I said I would be. Decker is a straight shooter. He asked for my help I said yes. I'm going to make sure nothing untoward happens to him," Cortez told him. Decker let out a silent sigh of relief.

"What do you know about Russell Cosgrove?" Decker asked suddenly, trying to force things back on track.

He wasn't about to put his gun away. Decker figured Delacorte had about ten guys waiting in the wings with guns just waiting for them to do something stupid.

"Of course, he's the lawyer for my good friend Jerry Contras. In fact, he's handling the merger of our companies. Why do you ask me about him?" Delacorte actually looked puzzled.

"Cosgrove was murdered last night on Scorpion Cay," Decker let it drop.

"And you suspect me," Delacorte said. It wasn't really a question.

"Nope. I just want to ask you a few questions. Such as why the merger? You don't make enough money smuggling cocaine these days?" Decker prodded him.

"I know you, Decker. You used to be Drug Enforcement. Now you are nothing, just a low-life peeper making his money catching cheating spouses," Delacorte spat.

"Wrong again, Miguel. I'm a homicide investigator working for the Scorpion Cay Police Department. I'll be polite and only ask you this once; did you kill or order the death of Russell Cosgrove?"

"Are you mad? Cosgrove had been working on the merger for weeks. Now a new attorney will have to take over and start again from the beginning. I would be most foolish to hit Mr. Cosgrove. You've wasted enough of my time, Decker. Leave and don't ever come back here," Delacorte replied icily.

"Thank you for your time," Decker backed towards the elevator. He noticed that Rafael was doing the same, his eyes darting in all directions, wondering where the attack would come from. We were almost to the elevator when he spoke.

"Decker. Beside the doors," Cortez whispered.

"Good idea, Pal," Decker stepped to the side. He hit the door button and they slid open with a ding. Two men stood inside the elevator holding pistols pointed towards the doorway. Rafael and Decker stabbed their pistols in and motioned for them to step out. We relieved them of their weapons as they stepped past us.

The ride back down to the lobby was uneventful. "You made a bad enemy there," Cortez said.

"What's one more," Decker grinned. Cortez shook his head.

The next stop on his list was the offices of Jerry Contras. Contras was old world Spanish. He was about a million miles above Delacorte on the social ladder. Maybe that was what was bothering me about the whole merger thing. What would Contras have to gain from taking on Delacorte as a partner? It had been nagging at him since Tanner had told Decker about it. Decker planned on doing more than just talking to Contras about it. He had made a couple of calls to friends still working with the government. Ones that Benny the Jet, nor Mitch Tanner were likely to know about. IRS guys that owed him a favors from his DEA days.

Decker planned on picking up complete financial statements about both companies and the men that owned them by close of business today. Of course he hadn't mentioned that fact to Delacorte or Contras, nor Cortez.

Of course they didn't go in with guns drawn like they had with Delacorte, but then Contras was a different sort of guy. He was much smoother, more refined. He also had no bad rap as a drug dealer. Jerry Contras was well respected within the Hispanic Community, a pillar. Totally the opposite of Miguel Delacorte.

Contras was definitely more refined. His hair was thinning and he looked a lot like Cheech Marin from Cheech and Chong. He was Old World Elegance, yet the feel of the street was evident in his mannerisms.

"Mr. Decker, Mr. Cortez, what may I do for you?" Contras greeted us.

"I need to ask you some questions about Russell Cosgrove and the work he was doing for you. You had heard that Mr. Cosgrove was murdered last night had you not?" Decker nodded. Contras was a far different animal than Delacorte and would have to be handled far more delicately.

"I had been notified yes. It pains me since Russell was not only my lawyer but a dear friend as well," Contras replied.

"Was Mr. Cosgrove working on anything specific for you?" Decker asked, knowing the answer but waiting to see what Contras had to say.

"Yes, he was. Mr. Cosgrove was working on a merger between my company and that of Miguel Delacorte. It would prove beneficial to us both," Contras replied smoothly. Almost too smoothly Decker felt.

"How would it have benefited you, Mr. Contras? Decker asked.

"Mister Delacorte has a lot of unused capital. That infusion of capital would allow me to expand my holdings and acquire more," Contras replied.

"And what would Mr. Delacorte get out of the deal?" he prodded.

"Legitimacy. He has a reputation, which is less

than sterling in the community. By making him a partner, it lends him a certain credibility within the community," Contras replied with a smile. Decker knew Contras was dancing around the real issue, and Contras knew he was dancing around it as well.

"According to Mr. Cosgrove's fiancé, he had uncovered some 'irregularities' while working on the merger. Do you know which company they might have come from?" Decker leaned forward.

"I know nothing of any irregularities," Contras replied, his face paling slightly.

"Really?" Decker leaned back.

"Russell said nothing to me," Contras replied. He was lying and they both knew it. The question was why? Decker decided not to pursue it for the moment.

"Given what's happened to Mr. Cosgrove, do you still plan to go through with the merger?" Decker asked.

"It's business, Mr. Decker. What happened to Russell came at a most unfortunate time, but as far as business is concerned, it is an inconvenience, nothing more. On a personal level I am deeply saddened by the death of my friend," Contras said. His last sentence was the only part of what he said that Decker believed. He stood up.

"I thank you for your time, Mr. Contras. I may be

back in touch later on with more questions," Decker shook hands with Contras. Rafael followed him out the door. They were both quiet until they were inside the elevator alone.

"He was lying," Rafael said.

"Yeah. I caught that. Do you think the irregularities are something Contras wants to keep hidden or Delacorte?" Decker shrugged.

"I'm not the detective. At this point in time, I will say that you cannot fully trust either of them. I especially would not trust Delacorte to not exact some measure of revenge for the way you braced him in his lair," Cortez replied.

"I agree. The question is which one of them will come after me first," Decker nodded. The rest of the trip to the lobby was made in silence.

Chapter Nine

Monica Sinclair leaned back in her chair. She had placed a call to New York after talking to Jessica Monroe. Monroe of course was not her real last name. It was Cochran. Monica looked at the pages on her desk. They told a lot different story about Jessica Cochran. Still, she felt for the girl. She had done a lot to reinvent herself after running away from the Mob.

Monica could also understand why the girl needed to know if her past had caught up with her. According to some friends on the NYPD, Jessica had nearly a million dollar bounty on her head. While Jessica knew that there was a contract out on her, Monica was willing to bet she didn't know how high a bounty was out on her.

She wondered if Decker knew what he might be going up against. Probably not. He was okay for a former fed. Not too hard on the eyes either. From what she had found out about him, Decker wasn't married, at least not anymore. His wife had left him back during the DEA days when he was working deep under cover.

Monica sighed. She had a suspect and victim who was a former prostitute and an ex fed with a lousy love life working the case for her. Glancing at the clock on the wall, she wondered what Decker was doing.

The street was almost deserted when they reached it. All the normal afternoon traffic had vanished from the streets. No cars, no pedestrians, even the stores looked deserted. "This doesn't look good," Decker said.

"Probably not. I gotta admit, *Jefe*, you draw trouble quicker than anybody I ever met," Cortez said.

"Which way do you think it'll come from?" Decker drew his pistol. A black SUV screeched around the corner, windows down, bristling with weapons.

"If I had to guess, that way," Cortez said, drawing and firing his gun. The big .44 Magnum Desert Eagle thundered loudly in the street, the noise of the blast sounding like artillery fire as it echoed off the buildings. A fist sized hole appeared in the rear door of the SUV and a body launched out the window missing a leg and splattering blood all over the place. Decker dived behind the car as bullets tore through the air like deadly lead hailstones. He stabbed the muzzle of the Sig-saur over the car and fired several rounds as glass shattered around him. At that point Decker was cursing soundly, knowing he was going to have to replace the windows and have a *lot* of body work done, feeling the car jump under the impact of automatic weapons fire. The SUV swung around the opposite corner and was gone. He felt a hand on his shoulder. "Getting out of here might be a good idea," Cortez said.

"Go ahead. I'm quasi official, and dealing with the Miami P.D. will be easier than dealing with the FDLE. Besides, Monica can get me sprung if it gets too bad," Decker stood up.

"I'll see if I can get a lead on those shooters. They got my suit dirty," Cortez said softly, then he was walking away. Decker almost felt sorry for those guys if Cortez found them. Then he looked at the mess that had been his car and didn't feel sorry for them at all.

When Miami Police arrived on the scene Decker was looking at his vintage 1965 Mustang and almost in tears. Decker had a feeling he would have to write the car off as a total loss. The windows were gone and the body on the street side looked like Swiss cheese. He also had a feeling that the Insurance Company was going to scream bloody murder about paying off to have it fixed. This was just not turning out to be a good day at all.

The first black and whites arrived on the scene within minutes and they didn't look at all friendly. Decker had a feeling that whoever was behind the shooting had a lot of clout. The uniforms didn't ask any questions at all, just confiscated his piece and read him his rights, and then it was a trip downtown in the back of a squad car. It didn't bother Decker *that* much since his wheels had been totaled.

The first swinging dick that came through the door was Detective Lloyd Saturday. Decker remembered him from his DEA days. He was an okay guy, not on the take. A rarity in the Vice division, an honest cop.

"Lloyd," Decker said by way of greeting as Saturday dropped heavily into the chair across from him.

"Samuel Decker, as I live and breathe! How have you been Sammy?" Lloyd asked him.

"Getting by, Lloyd. How about you?" Decker

asked, trying to project an image of relaxed nonchalance.

"Getting by, Sammy Boy, getting by. What's this I hear about your car getting shot up in front of Jerry Contras' place today?" he asked. Decker shrugged. Saturday knew the details as well as he did, there wasn't any need to add anything.

"Working were you?" he probed.

"You might say that. Official investigation on behalf of the Scorpion Cay Police Department. Investigating the murder of Russell Cosgrove last night," Decker replied.

"I heard about that. That kind of news, it travels fast," Lloyd replied. "So who would want to shoot at you, Sammy?"

"That's the question of the hour, Lloyd. However, I got no answers. I can tell you who I talked to today, but it won't prove anything. You know already I saw Contras. These guys were waiting for me to leave there. The only other person I spoke to was Miguel Delacorte. He didn't like what I asked him," Decker shrugged leaning back in his seat..

"Miguel Delacorte? You your usual charming self?" Lloyd asked.

"Ah heck Lloyd, I only know one way to be,"

Decker grinned.

"I can imagine. Old Balls to the Wall Decker. You went in with guns drawn and a smart ass attitude. Don't bother denying it, we've already looked at the surveillance footage from his office. You and Cortez did nothing more than talk to him, we knew that. However, there is a good chance that Delacorte took offense at your style of questioning," Saturday said.

"You think?" Decker shook his head.

"Benny the Jet has been nosing around ever since you been brought in. He's hoping we'll hold you," Saturday said.

"That is very interesting news. What did you tell him?" Decker asked.

"No evidence," Lloyd grinned.

"I bet he hated that," Decker smiled.

"You have no idea," Lloyd Saturday chuckled.

"So how long before you cut me loose?" Decker asked.

"How about now?"

"Now sounds really good," Decker smiled.

"Anything to fuck over Benny the Jet," Lloyd replied with a grin of his own.

Rafael was waiting outside when Decker walked

out of the police station. He was driving a black Mercedes Benz. Cortez was leaning against the fender as Decker walked down the stair. "What took you so long?" he smiled.

"Red tape, you know how that goes," Decker sighed.

"Yeah, 'bout like immigration," Rafael replied.

"You got it. Can you give me a ride home?" Decker asked.

"Somebody got to watch your back for you. I ain't got nothing else going on right now," he shrugged.

"Thanks," Decker nodded.

"You'd do the same for me," he smiled. He was right. Decker would. They both knew the rules and respected them, even though they had worked opposite sides of the street. They could trust one another to do exactly what they had said they would.

Together, they caught the evening ferry back to Scorpion Cay. Decker knew Monica would enjoy having Cortez around about as much as she liked having a shark in her swimming pool. Decker on the other hand, was happy to have Cortez watching his back.

Decker picked up his Harley at the dock and Rafael followed him back to his little beach house. Decker unlocked the doors and went inside, picking up his spare gun, a 9mm Browning Hi-Power. The Miami Police Department had held onto his Sig to run the ballistics on it. Given the caliber of the players in this case, there was no way he was going to run around unarmed while making a target of himself. Not even with Rafael watching his back.

By the time Decker got back to the door, Rafael was heading in lugging a large green duffel bag towards the door. "What's that?" Decker asked. Again he got that look from Cortez that made him wonder if the word stupid was tattooed on his forehead.

"Tools of the trade, Babe," he replied, grinning. In other words, a small arsenal that might contain anything up to and including a cruise missile. Rafael was a bit like a boy scout in that respect, he liked to be prepared.

"Fine. You set up shop and I'm gonna head for the station to chat with Monica and let her know I have a house guest," Decker sighed.

"Good luck," Rafe grinned.

"Yeah, right," Decker walked out the door.

Monica Sinclair was at her desk when Decker walked in. She looked sleep deprived and haggard. A steaming cup of coffee was sitting next to her as she read through some reports. He tapped lightly on the door and she waved him inside.

"So what have you got?" Monica asked, sounding every bit as tired as she looked. Decker had a feeling she had been up a lot longer than just twenty-four hours.

"Somebody willing to kill to keep us from finding out who was behind Cosgrove's death," Decker shook his head.

"You have my attention," Monica picked up the coffee and sipped it.

"Cortez and I spoke with both Delacorte and Contras this morning. After speaking with Contras, my car got shot up as we were leaving. Somebody greased the skids with Miami P.D. and got me kicked loose pretty quick. I was thinking that might have been you," Decker told her.

"It wasn't but it sure makes things look even more interesting. This whole Cosgrove case is turning into one giant jurisdictional cluster-fuck, Decker. It happened here on the Cay, but both the State Police and the Feds want to stick their noses and hands into it. Why do they want such a piece of this case?" Monica asked.

"Let me count the ways. A high-profile case, lots of publicity, a well-known drug smuggler trying to climb into bed with a well-respected Cuban American businessman with political ambitions; what's there that they wouldn't want to be a part of?" Decker asked sarcastically.

"Contras has political ambitions?" Monica seemed slightly surprised by that.

"Yeah and when I talked about Cosgrove's murder, he got very nervous. I think he and Delacorte both know a lot more than they were telling," Decker sat on the edge of the desk.

"I think you might be right. Jessica called earlier and said that the FDLE and the Feds had slapped a lockdown on Cosgrove's office. Nothing in and nothing out until they sifted through every file in the place," Monica said.

"Monica, this thing is big. Really big from the sound of it. Are you sure we should stay involved?" Decker asked softly. The ceiling fan turned quietly above them.

"I've been asking myself that very thing," Monica sighed, drinking some more coffee.

"What kind of answer have you come up with?" Decker asked, his voice soft.

"It happened here, on my watch, on my beat. I can't turn it over to anybody else. I have to clear this one,

Sam," Monica replied softly. Decker nodded, agreeing with her. She didn't clear this case; she would lose a lot of respect not only from the people on the island but from the state and federal authorities as well. If they cracked it before her, they would always be throwing it in her face, demeaning her with her failure. She needed to crack this case, and Decker knew he had to help her.

"Maybe not the best time to tell you, but I brought Cortez over to watch my back. Quasi-official or not, we pissed some people off today," Decker said.

"I figured that was going to happen. I hate the guy and everything he stands for, but I also know how you are. You'll stand by him and he'll stand by you and cover your back much more effectively than any of my force could. I don't like it but I'll allow it," Monica sighed leaning back in her chair.

"Thanks. I'll help you do this," Decker looked into her dark brown eyes.

"I'll try to come up with a suitable way to say thank you," Monica replied her voice suddenly husky. Decker wanted to kiss her badly right then, but it would have lacked decorum to kiss a superior officer in her office.

"You going to be busy tonight?" Monica asked, almost panting.

"Not unless I have an invitation to something?" Decker replied, his own breath coming hard.

"You're invited to my place around seven. Don't be late," Monica whispered.

"I won't," Decker said, struggling to get the words out.

Monica smiled and it was the most dazzling sight he had ever beheld. Decker stumbled as he turned and walked out of the office thinking of the promise that the night held.

Chapter Ten

"I thought you said you could handle this," the man said.

"I can," Benito Juarez replied.

"You better. I don't like them coming around and asking questions. Those kind of questions could prove embarrassing to us both."

"I'll take care of it boss. Decker won't get any closer. If he does, I will kill him myself," Benny the Jet replied.

"Remember those words, Benito. Pray that they don't return to haunt you," the man replied. Benny nodded.

"I have some people on it," Benny replied.

*****

Benny the Jet, aka Benito Juarez was sweating as he walked into the Parrot's Beak. Jimmy, the bartender automatically drew him a Budweiser from the tap and set it in front of him. "Thanks," Benny said. Jim nodded his head and then moved away to serve someone else. Benny sipped at his beer, even though he had a strong desire to gulp it down.

There was a lot of stuff going down on this piss-ant island. More than he had ever thought possible. Jerry Cosgrove was certainly a catalyst that was for sure. The big question was why was he such a catalyst? What had Cosgrove known that was responsible for his death?

Benny wanted to know. He could profit from that kind of information. There were a lot of players in the game. Delacorte, Contras, anyone they might have hired. He shook his head. There was even his own boss who had not yet popped up on anybody's radar yet. So much could happen before it was all over.

Decker was worn out when he walked out of the police station. It had been a long damn day and it wasn't over yet by any means. There was something in the whole ratted tangle that he wasn't seeing. What was it? Who was

behind it all? What had Russell Cosgrove uncovered that

somebody was willing to kill to conceal? All he had was a

lot of questions and no answers. Decker hated that. Still,

he had upset somebody's apple cart, which was why the

shooters had made their try in Miami. The question of the

moment was would they follow him here to Scorpion Cay?

The answer had to lie in the financial records

pertaining to the merger. Somehow he had to find a way to

get a hold of them. The Treasury boys had already locked

Cosgrove's office down tight. Decker's only hope would

be if Cosgrove had brought copies home with him to work

on. There was only one way to find out about that. Decker

would have to talk to Jessica again. He wasn't sure how

she would feel about going back to the house. He shook his

head as he climbed back onto his Harley and kick-started it

to life.

There were too damn many questions and nothing

in the way of answers in sight. Decker headed back over to

Nora Santiago's house to have a chat with Jessica Monroe.

He was about halfway across the island to Nora's

place when he noticed the plain white pick-up truck on his

tail. They had just gotten on a fairly remote section of road when he heard the engine of the pick-up roar as the driver stomped on the gas. Decker leaned over the handlebars working the throttle to send the Harley speeding ahead.

Decker glanced in his rearview mirror and noticed that despite the fact that the Harley was going near its top speed the grill of the pickup was growing larger. He had to get off the road, but to try it at his current speed would be suicide, yet slowing down would get him killed just as quickly by the speeding truck. Some days it just really sucked to be him!

Decker reached under his jacket and drew the Browning left handed. The hammer was up over a loaded chamber and the safety was off. Decker thrust his arm behind him and started squeezing the trigger. A couple of shots were lucky and the windshield spider-webbed under the impact of the 124-grain Hydroshok bullets. The pick-up swerved and slowed, dropping back dramatically. This was his one chance!

Decker eased off the throttle, shifting down and slowing the Harley as quick as he could. Decker spotted an opening at the side of the road and pulled off onto a dirt trail, hearing the truck slam on its brakes. Damn, he had been hoping that he had at least hurt the driver! Luck just wasn't on his side!

Decker took the Harley over a small hill and killed the engine, skidding to a halt in the dirt. He put down the kickstand and switched the Browning to his right hand. He still had about half a fourteen round magazine in it and one spare on under his right armpit. Decker hoped it would be enough.

The air had gone silent and Decker realized that the driver of the truck had shut off his engine as well. He felt a smile stretch across his lips. It was down to the two of them now. The Hunter and the hunted. The bad part was, the guy who thought he was the hunter was actually the hunted!

Decker was of course giving himself credit for becoming the hunter when a bullet cut the air above his head and sent him diving for cover. Whoever was in the truck was good. They had gotten out and managed to slip into the trees that bordered the road. Decker cursed his own carelessness as he hugged the sand and elephant grass. Shit! It looked like he was still the hunted. This would never do.

Decker crab-crawled his way to the left, figuring his assailant would come from that side. His assailant would be expecting Decker to go the other way and try to flank him. He hoped. His palm was sweaty on the finger-grooved pachmayer grip of the Browning, but Decker knew that the Hogue grips wouldn't allow the gun to slip. That was why he had put them on it many years ago.

Decker kept an eye on the tree line and finally spotted him. A large Hispanic, but nobody he recognized. Decker eased the muzzle of the Browning 9mm over the top of the hill and lined up the sights. He slowed his breathing, relaxing into what was about to happen, following the target as it moved.

The person stalking him was no longer a man, just a target. Cold and impersonal. Decker's finger tightened on the trigger and the Browning roared in his fist. The target's head exploded as the 9mm projectile punched through his skull.

Decker waited a few moments longer, just to make sure that there were no other gunners lying in wait. He unclipped his cellular phone and dialed Monica Sinclair.

"Sinclair," her voice answered.

"Monica, somebody just tried to kill me," Decker told her, keeping his voice level.

"Where are you?" she asked, her voice tight with concern.

"Out on Coconut Run, about halfway across it. You should be able to spot the guy's white pick-up truck. I'm moving down to check the body," Decker started slowly down the hill. He was pretty sure nobody else was lurking about, but it never hurt to be careful.

This case was getting nastier by the minute. The dead guy was nobody he had ever seen before but that didn't mean much. There were a lot of guns for hire in Little Havana that Decker had never met.

It didn't take long for the cops to converge on Coconut Run and pretty soon the whole place was full of flashing Mars lights. Decker had time to smoke a couple of cigarettes and regain his composure before Monica approached him. She had insisted on micro-managing her people as they went about securing the crime scene. Some of it was to keep them on their toes, but a big part of it was to get Monica's own emotions under control. She also knew better than to come at him with a full head of anger and steam about something that wasn't his fault. After all, Decker didn't tell the asshole to try and kill him. He had just reacted to the situation.

He still wanted to get to Jessica Monroe and get out to the house she and Russell Cosgrove had shared. Decker had a gut feeling that the answers were there if he could just find them. Now at least, his gut was telling him where to look.

"You okay?" Monica asked finally as she appeared by his side. Decker nodded without speaking, his eyes still looking into the distance. "Tell me what happened," she gently prodded.

Decker told her what had happened from the beginning and she listened quietly, interrupting briefly with an occasional question to clarify some detail or another. Finally, Monica sighed. She looked up at him with those beautiful brown eyes, all seriousness and sincerity. "I'm sorry I got you involved in this," Monica said softly.

"No you're not. You're just sorry it's put a target on my chest. I'm a means to an end, Monica. I know that. You want this case cracked and you know I'm the best shot at it you've got. I'm out front drawing the fire while you do your thing quietly in the background. That's okay though. I'm used to it. It goes with the territory," Decker shrugged.

"Sam, no that's—" she started.

"Monica, I know the score. I've known it since you had me taken out to Cosgrove's house. Sure, we're friends. Good friends. Don't try to play me for a fool. I may speak with a Deep South accent, but that for damn sure doesn't make me stupid. That's something you Yankees tend to forget," Decker said, the words sounding harsher than he had intended.

It was a mistake and he knew it as soon as the words left his mouth. The caring and compassion in her eyes vanished, replaced with the icy cop stare. Whatever he might have had with Monica, he was pretty sure it ended right there.

"You son of a bitch!" she hissed, her face turning red with anger.

"Thanks for noticing," Decker said, making the situation even worse.

"Decker, you can stay on the case, but now it's totally professional. Don't bother stopping by for dinner. That invitation has been rescinded. Forever," she said with an air of finality.

"Fine," he sighed, turning and heading for his bike. Decker figured he had just lost something that could have been a really good part of his future. Oh well, that's the way it goes. He kick started the Harley and then he headed for his house. Decker wanted to fill Cortez in on what had happened. They had pissed off more than just Monica today.

*****

Benny the Jet watched as the men filed off the sea

plane. He had agreed to get them onto the island without being seen. His employer had sent them to take out Decker. Decker seemed to be getting close. Benny smiled as Ed Navarro stepped off the plane. He and Ed went way back, working together to move high grade cocaine for the Columbian Cartels and keeping it out of the hands of the DEA and local law enforcement. Navarro stood about six foot six and weighed in close to 250 lbs of solid muscle. His short black hair was plastered to his head with some sort of oil and his pencil thin mustache gleamed in the sunlight.

"Benito, Amigo. How's it hanging?" Navarro asked. He extended his hand and Benny was very aware of the thickly corded muscle and power in those arms. Cautiously, Benny accepted the hand and shook it. He felt a tickle of fear at the base of his spine, knowing that Navarro could kill him quicker than he could blink.

"Hanging loose, Amigo. Long time no see," Benny grinned, trying to cover what he was feeling. Navarro could probably smell his fear though. Eduardo Navarro was a professional soldier and a professional assassin. Navarro was followed off the plane by four other men.

"You have us a place to operate from?" Navarro asked.

"Of course, Ed. Have I ever let you down?" Benny asked.

"Not so far," Navarro said quietly, and once more Benny felt the icy finger of fear stroke his spine. Navarro had an unsettling presence. Only one other man he knew affected him the same way. Sam Decker. Like Navarro, Decker had the eyes of a predator. Benny felt a chill race down his spine. It would be interesting watching Navarro go up against Decker. He wondered which one would survive.

*****

"You really know how to make friends and influence people," Rafael Cortez shook his head as Decker relayed him the events of the past hour, including the blow up with Monica.

"What can I say, it's one of my many talents," Decker shrugged. Cortez snorted derisively.

"Call it what you will, Jefe you got problems. You got people you don't even know trying to kill you to keep you off of this thing," Cortez shook his head.

"Just my winning personality I guess. You up for a ride out to Cosgrove's house?" Decker was refilling the magazine of his Browning.

"Sounds like it might be fun," Rafe smiled.

"You never know," Decker grinned.

"I'll drive," Rafael nodded, snatching up his green canvas duffle bag. Decker slapped the magazine back in his pistol and followed him out the door. He used his cell to call Jessica Monroe and tell her they would be by in just a few minutes to pick her up.

Chapter Eleven

Nora Santiago followed Jessica out of the house a worried expression on her face. She leaned into the car as Jessica climbed inside and looked me in the eye. "Should you really be doing this?" she asked, concern evident in both her voice and expression. Nora was good people. She had always been a friend.

"Don't have much choice. We need to go through his papers and she's the only one with the authority to let us into the house," Decker replied soberly.

"It's okay, Nora. I trust Mr. Decker," Jessica Monroe said from the seat behind him.

"Rafael, take care of them both," Nora said, looking pointedly at Cortez. Until this moment, Decker had no idea they even knew each other.

"I will," Cortez said from the driver's seat. Nora shook her head and he put the car in gear.

"You and Nora know each other?" Decker asked, his curiosity getting the better of him.

"Yes," Cortez replied, saying nothing further. His silence spoke volumes. Decker knew he would get no farther asking him about Nora Santiago. They rode in silence to Russell Cosgrove's house. Decker guessed it was really Jessica's house now. Jessica sat quietly in the back seat, and he could only guess how this was making her feel. She was returning to the house she had shared with the man she loved. The man that had been murdered twenty-four hours before.

Decker's mind wandered back to his last conversation with Monica. He knew he should call and apologize, but his own stubborn pride kept him from doing so. Decker's words had been harsh, but he had just been shot at repeatedly. She should have had the decency to treat him with respect, rather than feed him a line of bullshit deep enough to swim in. It wasn't about him, though. It was about the case.

Jessica Monroe had asked his help in finding Russell Cosgrove's killer. Monica had asked the same. Decker had respected Cosgrove. He felt like he owed it to

Cosgrove to find out who had killed him and why.

The ride across the island to Cosgrove's house was a silent one except for the salsa music blasting out of the speakers of Rafael's car. None of them felt much like talking though Decker had a number of questions he wanted to ask. However, it really wasn't the time for them. They were rolling up on the house that Jessica Monroe had shared with Russell Cosgrove when Decker noticed the big black Lincoln Towncar in the driveway.

"Decker," Rafael's voice broke through Decker's reverie as he spoke his name. Decker noticed that the car was slowing as he looked up, and his hand drifted automatically to the butt of the Browning at his hip.

"Recognize that car?" Decker glanced over the seat at Jessica, nodding his head to indicate the one he was talking about.

"No I don't," Jessica replied softly, her voice trembling with fear. Coming back to this house had been hard enough for her to begin with. Her final memories of it had not been pleasant. Decker's hand was gripping the butt of his Browning as Rafael's car rolled to a stop and he stepped out onto the crushed shell drive.

Rafael had stepped from the driver's side, a twelve-gauge pump appearing as if by magic in his hands. The muzzle of the shotgun covered the black Lincoln Towncar. "Stay in the car," Decker told Jessica as he stepped closer to the Lincoln.

The Browning was fully extended and the hammer was drawn back to full cock when one of the darkly tinted windows slid silently down. "Can I help you?" a calm voice asked from inside the Lincoln. It was a lot calmer than Decker would have been with a couple of guns aimed at him.

"Care to tell us who you are?" Decker's finger was tight against the trigger. He had been shot at enough for one day. It was beginning to make him cranky. The driver's door swung open and the muzzle of Rafael's shotgun swung towards it, the sound of the shell being racked into the chamber amazingly loud.

"Slowly," Rafael said, his voice soft, yet commanding. Slowly a man in a chauffer's uniform climbed out and moved slowly and carefully around the Lincoln to the rear passenger door with the open window. The chauffer opened the door. Jason Marshall stepped out. Decker recognized him immediately from multiple stories that had appeared in the Miami Herald, photos included.

"Mr. Marshall," Jessica said from behind him. Decker shot a quick glance over his shoulder. Jessica had not followed orders and was standing outside the car. He felt the muscles in his shoulders bunch beneath his shirt as he swung the pistol towards Marshall's chest. Jason Marshall was one of Russell Cosgrove's partners. Decker wondered what the hell he was doing in front of Cosgrove's house.

"Jessica, I am so sorry about Russ. I came out to see if there was anything I could do," Marshall told her.

"Like what?" Decker asked. He didn't like this guy on sight. Marshall was about five foot nine, reddish hair going to gray, his body going to fat. He weighed 260 lbs if he weighed an ounce. Decker had a feeling he was one of the many who had made a living feeding off the great guy that Russell Cosgrove had been.

"How are you Jessica? Do you have enough money to get by with?" Marshall asked, ignoring me. Decker felt an instant dislike wash over him. He jammed the muzzle of the Browning up under Marshall's chin.

"I'll ask the questions," Decker said, holding his gaze unblinkingly, even as they focused on him with a gaze of pure evil.

"You are?" Marshall asked, nonplused.

"Samuel Decker, Private Investigator," he replied. Decker wasn't sure what kind of reaction he was expecting.

Marshall laughing outrageously certainly wasn't it.

"You're Decker?" he gasped after several minutes. Decker had no idea that his erstwhile hostage found him so amusing.

"Yeah," Decker replied. Marshall continued to laugh and it was really beginning to irk him. Rafael could see it as well and he prodded the man with the shotgun, causing the chauffer to tense up.

"I'm sorry, Mr. Decker. Based on your reputation I rather expected you to have two horns and a tail," Marshall chuckled.

"Sorry to disappoint," Decker said, though he really wasn't. Marshall just didn't know enough about him to know that there was a darker side just below the surface. "What do you really want?"

"Jessica, Russell was working on some personal items for me. I was wondering if I could go through his papers and get mine," Marshall said, ignoring me.

"The police took all of Russell's work," Jessica said and Decker offered a silent prayer of thanks to whatever gods might be listening. Jessica was quick. Even she didn't buy Marshall's story. A cloud passed over Marshall's face.

"Everything?" he asked, but it came out more like

the sibilant hiss of a snake.

"That's right," Decker cut in. "I brought Jessica out so that she could pick up some personal items she might be needing." Marshall turned his eyes back to Decker's and he could see the rage behind the cool gaze. Marshall hid it well however.

"I see. I guess then we should be heading back to the Ferry dock if we wish to return to the mainland today," Marshall said.

"Probably so," Decker lowered the Browning.

"Thank you, that was most annoying," Marshall said with a smile so oily Decker almost thought a tanker had dumped its load on the island.

"Not nearly so annoying as it could have been," Decker smiled. Marshall looked at him for a long moment.

"I suppose you're right," he nodded. Then Marshall turned and walked back to the Lincoln and climbed inside. The chauffer shot Decker and Cortez a dirty look as he closed the door behind him and then returned to the driver's seat and started the engine. Moments later, the Lincoln was gone.

"You buy any of that?" Rafael asked, shaking his head.

"Not one bit," Decker replied as he started towards

the house.

"Why was he really here?"

"That's the question, isn't it?" Decker shrugged.

"Has any one ever told you that you can be really annoying?" Jessica asked.

"All the time," Decker grinned.

"He excels at it," Rafe added nodding.

"Everybody needs to be good at something," Decker holstered his gun. The three of them walked to the house and Decker was the first to notice that the door was slightly open. He drew his pistol and shot Rafe a look. Cortez's own gun was out and he nodded his understanding.

"What's going on?" Jessica asked, her confusion filling her face. Decker raised a finger up over his lips quieting her. He was pretty sure that there was nobody inside, but it never hurt to be sure. Decker motioned for her to wait and gently pushed the door open and stepped inside. Rafael had already started around to the back door.

The inside of the house was as silent as a tomb if you'll pardon the pun, since that was what the place had become when Russell Cosgrove was murdered. Decker's Browning led the way as he moved through the place, going room to room. Rafael would wait outside so they didn't accidentally shoot each other before the place was cleared. Decker checked it all, under beds, in closets, nothing. He was pretty sure that Marshall and his boy had already been through the place before they got there, but it never hurt to make sure.

"Anything out of place?" Decker asked Jessica after waving her inside. Rafael was already in the kitchen fixing some sort of health drink concoction.

"Nothing I can see right off hand," Jessica brushed a stray lock of blond hair back from her face. Her pale blue eyes bored into his.

"How long to find out?" Decker asked, the whir of the blender slightly distracting.

"For me to check everything? About an hour," Jessica shrugged.

"Start looking," Decker said, watching as she moved away. It was hard not to watch. Jessica exuded a potent sexuality that was hard to ignore, despite his best efforts. Rafael looked at him and grinned from ear to ear.

"It is hard, is it not?" he asked, his grin spreading across his face.

"What?" Decker asked, trying to look puzzled even though he knew what Cortez meant.

"Working for such a beautiful woman and trying not to notice," he grinned.

"Yeah," Decker sighed, knowing an honest answer was the best one.

"I take it your friend Monica would not approve?" Rafael asked, his eyes twinkling with suppressed mischief.

"You might say that," Decker agreed.

Chapter Twelve

It actually took less than an hour for Jessica to discover that the house had been searched and quite thoroughly at that. Even her computer had been searched, her novel read. Tears were welling in her eyes as she spoke of the feeling of violation. Decker had a feeling that the novel being read hit her harder than Russell Cosgrove being killed.

While nothing was missing, the fact that Marshall had searched so thoroughly told him that there was more to what Marshall wanted than he was willing to admit. Decker planned on taking a much closer look at

Jason Marshall as soon as possible. He had a feeling that Tanner's pet Treasury man could tell him a lot about Marshall if he asked the right questions. You never knew with the Feds, though, especially that bunch over at Treasury. They were sneaky bastards

Decker pulled out his cell phone and punched in Mitch Tanner's number. "Tanner," the answer came back in an instant.

"Hey Mitch, what can you find out about Jason Marshall from your pet treasury agent?" Decker ran his fingers through his sweat-soaked hair.

"I'll find out and let you know. Oh, by the way Sam, Treasury says one of their boys went missing last night about the time Cosgrove got whacked," Tanner said.

"Got a description?" Decker asked, suddenly very curious. He listened quietly as Tanner described the dead man he had found in the house of Mama Celeste.

"He's not missing anymore, Mitch. I found his body last night," Decker sighed.

"Your police chief can't keep us out of this case anymore, Sam," Tanner said softly. Monica

"I'll let you be the one to tell her that," Decker said, breaking the connection.

"Trouble?" Cortez asked.

"Loads of it," Decker sighed. He knew what he had to do next and he didn't like it even a little bit. He punched in Sinclair's number.

"What do you want, Decker?" Monica Sinclair's voice sliced into his ear.

"Got more bad news for you. The dead guy at Mama Celeste's house was Treasury Department. FDLE will be moving in to cover that part of this case," Decker told her.

"Shit!"

"Yeah that was my thought as well," Decker said. He looked around, eyeing the land around Jessica's house.

"Watch your ass, Decker. I got word that Benny the Jet met some heavy hitters on a remote section of beach today. They flew in by amphibious plane," Monica warned.

"Got it boss. I'll be in touch," Decker broke the connection and looked at Cortez. "We need to get her out of here and I mean right now."

"What's up, Jefe?" Cortez turned to face him.

"Benny brought in some big guns. We need to get her to safety and get ready," Decker wiped the sweat from his forehead.

"Amigo I was born ready," Cortez grinned. They headed for the car. Jessica carried a folder filled with cd-rom discs.

"What's on the discs?" Decker finally asked, surprising Jessica with the question.

"My novel," Jessica said clutching them tightly.

"Could Russell have hidden anything on the discs?" Decker turned to look at her.

"I guess he could have. I haven't looked over the early chapters in awhile," Jessica shrugged.

"Monica say who Benny brought in?" Cortez asked, seemingly at ease even as his eyes scanned the road and the surroundings.

"Nope, just that they were heavy hitters," Decker shook his head.

"Be nice to know who we had going up against us," Cortez smiled.

"That it would, Rafe. Honestly though, you think it would make a difference?" Decker eyed his friend.

"It might. Make it easier to prepare anyway," Cortez shook his head.

*****

Ed Navarro looked around the safehouse that Benny the Jet had rented for them. The place was small, but that didn't really matter all that much. They wouldn't be on the

island that long. Just long enough to kill one very nosey
private investigator named Sam Decker. Navarro grinned
at the thought.

He knew Decker from years past. Decker had given
him a line of bullet scars that traversed his torso from left
to right. Scars that pained him when the weather changed.
It would give him a great deal of pleasure to pull the
trigger on the former DEA agent.

*****

Mitch Tanner had brought the ferry over to Scorpion
Cay this trip, so he was driving an official FDLE car this
trip. He had tried calling Benito Juarez, but Benny the Jet
wasn't answering his cell phone. That didn't really surprise
Tanner though. Benny had been vanishing off and on since
they had first gotten the call to head over to Scorpion Cay
before Russell Cosgrove had gotten assassinated. More
and more that was how he was looking at the Cosgrove
case, as an assassination. Somebody didn't want whatever
Cosgrove had discovered to be made public and was
willing to kill to keep it covered up.

The big question was who? Of course knowing
what Cosgrove had found would be a big help in finding
the who. He shook his head. He hated the fact that he

had brought Decker into it, especially with Benny the Jet running around muddying up the water, but he had no choice. There was no love lost between Decker and Juarez, so if anything happened to Benny, he, Tanner, had deniability.

Tanner shook out a cigarette and lit it as he headed for the Scorpion Cay Police Station. He wasn't looking forward to butting heads with Monica Sinclair again. She was some woman all right. She seemed to deserve every bit of the reputation that had followed her from New York City of being a real ball buster. Still, Decker seemed to like and respect her.

Tanner finished his cigarette as he pulled into the parking lot and found a space. He took care to stub it out in the rental's ashtray rather than toss the butt on the lot and maybe set the chief off again. He needed her to work with him on this case if they were to solve it. Tanner opened the door and stepped out of the car as the first shot rang out. His rear window shattered and Tanner threw himself to the ground, scrambling for cover as another bullet blasted a chunk of concrete from the curb. Using the car as a shield he drew his Rugar P-85 from its holster on his hip.

Another shot rang out from the distance and the windshield of his rental exploded in a shower of glass fragments. Try as he might, he couldn't see where the shots were coming from. The door of the police station opened and he shouted, "Get back inside!" The door slammed closed and then shattered as another hi-powered bullet punched through it.

Silence settled over the parking lot, the only sound the occasional tinkle of broken glass falling to the pavement and the ticking of the cooling engine of his car. Tanner pulled out his phone and dialed Monica Sinclair.

"Sinclair," her voice came back in his ear. Tanner sighed.

"Anybody in there hurt?" Tanner rose up, searching the horizon for some sign of the shooter.

"Not physically, but I got a couple of guys that shit their pants. You hit?" Sinclair asked.

"Nope, but my suit is never going to be the same. I think the shooter is gone. I'm coming in," Tanner had his feet beneath him now.

"We've got a counter sniper on the roof so come ahead. That dickhead shoots again, we'll be shooting back," Sinclair said. Tanner grinned, flipped his phone shut and ran for the door of the police station.

Nobody shot at him and he was thankful for it. Gasping for breath, Tanner decided that maybe he should cut back on the cigarettes. Decker had been right, smoking had almost gotten him killed. Holstering his Pistol, he looked up to see Monica Sinclair heading down the hall towards him. She did not look happy.

"Hello Chief Sinclair. I wish I had better news," Tanner shook his head.

"Decker already told me. Right now though, I think you got bigger problems," She tossed her hair back.

"Yeah, me too," Tanner agreed.

"Know where Benny is right now?" Monica held his gaze.

"He's not answering his phone," Tanner sighed.

"I'm putting out a BOLO on him. I want that son of a bitch in a cage where I can keep an eye on him," Monica spun away, heading for the radio room. Tanner watched her for a long moment and then followed her. He wanted to see if she would really do it.

*****

Sam Decker eased out of the car a block away from his house. He held an Uzi submachine gun in both fists as he slipped behind the neighbor's house and moved along the alley to the back of his own place. He and Cortez had dropped Jessica off at Nora Santiago's again before coming back here. The Uzi might have been overkill, but Benny the Jet knew where he lived. Decker planned on taking no chances.

Sweat was beading on his forehead and running into his eyes as he approached the back of the house. Something moved near the back door. Decker adjusted his grip on the Uzi and stepped into the open. A guy wearing military fatigues was fooling with his gas meter. Decker fired a three-round burst, dropping the man in his tracks. Slowly he approached the man. Cortez appeared from the front of the house, his big .44 Magnum leveled.

"How will the gas company feel about you shooting their meter man?" Cortez looked around the yard.

"They read the meter last week. He breathing?" Decker kept the Uzi pointed at the body as he drew closer.

"Doesn't appear to be. Want me to shoot him again to be sure?" Cortez stepped closer.

"Put one in his leg, I think he might be wearing a vest," Decker called back. Cortez thumbed back the hammer of the .44 with a loud click. The man rolled, guns coming into his fists. Cortez and Decker both fired as one and the man's head exploded. Guns fell from suddenly nerveless fingers and the body flopped to the ground.

"This time, he is dead Amigo," Cortez smiled.

"Yeah, let's see what he was playing with at the gas meter," Decker said. He'd check the body for identification in a minute, though he really didn't expect to find any.

"Got any friends good with explosives?" Cortez asked, stepping back from the meter.

"What?" Decker squinted, looking at it more closely.

Then he saw the brick of clay-like substance with wires running into it. "Shit. Let's get out of here!" They moved back to the alley and Decker dialed Mitch Tanner on his cell phone.

"Tanner," came the reply.

"Get some of your bomb squad boys over to my place really quick. Also tell Monica that I've got a dead man laying real close to the bomb attached to my gas meter," Decker shook his head.

"Here, you might want to tell her that last part yourself," Tanner said. A heartbeat later Monica's voice was in his ear.

"What now, Decker?" she asked, her voice sounding strained.

"I came home and caught somebody wiring a bomb to my gas meter. He didn't survive, but the bomb is still on the meter," Decker sighed.

"Tanner's on a land line for a bomb squad out of Miami-Dade Metro. I'm beginning to think you're not very well liked," Monica sighed.

"Me too," Decker said, breaking the connection. He looked at Cortez. "Bomb Squad is on the way. So who do you think is behind this?"

"Not Delacorte's style. He'd just come in shooting. I can only think of one person that dislikes you enough to hire a mercenary to take you out," Cortez shrugged.

"Benny the Jet," Decker sighed.

Chapter Thirteen

The four of them sat in a dark corner booth of The Parrot's Beak; Decker, Cortez, Tanner, and Sinclair. Several more FLDE agents had been called in to help hunt for Benito Juarez. Those agents were scouring the island. The waitress dropped off a tray of drinks and Decker handed her a fifty dollar bill. "Keep it," he said as she smiled her thanks. He knew that Tina was working hard to raise her five year old son. She needed the money.

"Big spender," Monica smiled at him. The smile surprised him and made him feel very happy.

"She has a kid. She deserves any breaks she can get," Decker shrugged, slightly embarrassed.

"You are too soft, Amigo," Cortez shook his head.

"Think you can get me a date?" Tanner asked, watching Tina depart.

"She's half your age, Mitch," Monica laughed.

"I know that. Guess it's wishful thinking on my part," Tanner nodded his head, grinning.

"Most likely," Decker laughed.

"Time to get down to business, guys," Monica Sinclair set her beer on the table.

"Yeah, it is," Decker nodded, agreeing with her.

"I'm fairly certain and ballistics back it up that the same shooter shot at Jessica in the hotel last night as well as shooting at Mitch this afternoon," Monica said.

"No argument there," Mitch Tanner took a sip of his beer.

"You figure Benny the Jet as the shooter?" Cortez took a pull from his Corona and set it on the table.

"Yeah, we do," Monica took another sip of her beer.

"So who the hell is Benny working for?" Decker leaned back in his seat.

"I'm guessing Marshall," Cortez nodded.

"You find out anything about him?" Decker looked at Tanner.

"Not yet. I've got people digging though," Tanner leaned back in his chair.

"Benny escorted some heavy hitters in at a remote location earlier this afternoon," Monica took a sip of her beer. Her leg had edged closer to Decker and was pressing against his leg now.

"Any idea who they were?" Decker looked at her.

"I'd say that the dead guy behind your house was one of them," Cortez set his bottle on the table.

"No arguments there," Decker shrugged.

"I think we all agree on that point," Monica said softly.

"So where the hell is Benny and why was he shooting at me?" Tanner took a sip of beer as he looked around the table.

"Obviously you were starting to get close to something," Decker sighed.

"He really is as bad as they say isn't he?" Tanner asked, looking around the table reading their faces.

"Yeah," Decker said quietly.

"So what do we know or think we know?" Monica asked.

"We know somebody killed Cosgrove for what he found out, but we don't know what he found which would likely tell us who," Decker took a pull on his Killian's Red.

"We're fairly certain that Benny the Jet tried to hit Jessica Monroe and me," Mitch Tanner added, still watching the young waitress.

"Delacorte tried to hit you in Miami because you pissed him off. I think someone else is behind the attempts here," Cortez added.

"Be nice to know who Benny is working for," Decker sat his empty bottle down.

"That would be a place to start," Tanner nodded.

"Finding Benny would be a better place to start," Monica said.

"Island ain't too big, so that shouldn't be too hard, not with all of the FDLE boys combing the place for him," Cortez drained the rest of his beer.

"Benny's like a cockroach, he could be hiding anywhere," Decker shook his head.

"The people he brought in got to be staying somewhere, and they likely wouldn't stay out in the open,' Cortez signaled the waitress for another round.

"I'll check with all the realtors, see if anything has been rented out in the last two days," Monica sipped her own drink.

"I'll have my boys start a door to door search. Benny may not be with them, he might have a squeeze here on the island," Tanner nodded, watching Tina return with a tray full of drinks. "I think I'm in love," he sighed.

"More than likely lust," Decker frowned.

"Love, lust, not that much difference between the two," Tanner grinned.

"Cynical attitude," Monica shook her head. Decker

waited until Tina had departed and gave Tanner a hard look.

"What?" Tanner asked.

"Tina is good people, Mitch. Don't fuck with her," Decker kept his voice pitched low and soft.

"I would also take exception if anyone forced their attentions on the young lady," Cortez said quietly.

"Listen both of you, she's hot, but I ain't Benny," Tanner held up his hands.

"Boys, settle down. Y'all got too much testosterone flowing round this table. You got me afraid of getting pregnant just from sitting near y'all," Monica cut in, speaking with a deep southern drawl that failed to hide her New York accent.

Decker grinned. "I think I might know how to find Benny."

"How?" Monica asked.

"Mama Celeste," Decker grinned.

"The Voodoo Priestess?" Cortez asked, setting his bottle on the table.

"You know her?" Decker raised his eyebrows.

"I know of her. Everyone in Little Havana does," Cortez said quietly.

Decker's cell phone picked then to ring and he flipped it open. "Decker," he held it to his ear.

"Mr. Decker, I think I found something. I was going through my computer discs and found one that isn't mine," Jessica Monroe's voice said in his ear.

"Meet us in Monica's office," Decker said then flipped the phone closed. He looked at Tanner. "We have to go now. I'll call you when we have something. Monica we need to get to the station," Decker stood up. Monica and Cortez followed suit.

"I'll finish my drink," Tanner nodded. Decker looked at him, feeling uneasy.

"Remember what I said about Tina," Decker said, giving Tanner a hard look. Tanner appeared unfazed.

"Hurt the girl in any way and the sharks will be the only ones who know where you went," Cortez said softly, smiling. Tanner paled but remained seated as they walked out.

"You think he's going to try and force himself on the waitress?" Rafael asked when they were outside.

"Maybe. He used to be a good cop, but I don't know how long he's been working with Benny," Decker shook his head.

"Do I want to hear this conversation?" Monica asked shaking her head.

"Probably not. If anything happens to Tina, Tanner will just disappear," Decker replied quietly.

"Oddly enough, I have no problem with that," Monica shrugged.

"Decker, I knew there was something I liked about this woman," Cortez grinned.

"Mister, you ain't as bad as you think you are," Monica eyed him.

"Yes he is," Decker said.

"So what was the phone call about?" Monica asked.

"Jessica Monroe found something. A computer disc that wasn't hers and a possible clue as to why Russell Cosgrove was murdered," Decker explained.

"A clue would be a good thing. It might even give us motive. So why not include Tanner?" Monica asked.

"I don't trust him," Decker shrugged.

"Because of his comments about the waitress," Monica said. It wasn't a question.

"Exactly," Decker shrugged.

"Men," Monica shook her head.

*****

"We need to go to the station," Jessica told Nora Santiago.

"Not a problem since my husband is home with the

kids," Nora smiled. She looked at her husband. "Baby, I gotta go to work," Nora smiled.

"Be careful, Nora. I've been hearing things about some big trouble on the island," Diego Santiago said softly, his eyes searching his wife's. Jessica had seen that same look in Russell's eyes. Nora Santiago was a lucky woman. She had a man that truly loved her. Nora stayed in plain clothes, but slipped into a shoulder holster and a light weight jacket, then slipped her pistol into place.

"Time to go," Nora smiled at Jessica, then she leaned over and gave her husband a deep kiss that left Jessica feeling almost embarrassed to have witnessed it.

The afternoon air was still, the heat hanging over the island almost like a shroud. Sweat beaded immediately on Jessica's forehead as she stepped out into the heat. She was thankful for the white cotton sundress she had slipped on before she had called Decker. She had also taken time to make a couple of copies of the strange disc. She hadn't looked at the contents, but she knew it wasn't hers.

Nora Santiago opened the door of the marked police car for her and Jessica smiled in return as she climbed inside it. Jessica liked the young Cuban policewoman. Nora had shown her more kindness than she had seen in years from another woman. Her family was absolutely delightful. Nora put the car in gear and backed out of the driveway and onto the street, then she shifted to drive and stepped on the gas.

"Has Decker made any progress?" Nora asked as she turned a corner.

"He didn't say. Hopefully this CD will shed some light on who killed Russell," Jessica shook her head. The police car had moved out onto the main thoroughfare that ran from one end of the island to the other. Nora had goosed the speed up when suddenly two black SUV's boxed the police car in.

"Get down!" Nora shouted as one of the big SUV's slammed into the driver's side sending them towards the guard rail. Nora fought for control with one hand as she drew her service automatic with the other. The rear windshield exploded inward, showering both women with glass.

Jessica couldn't help herself, she started to scream. She heard the booming report of Nora's gun. Jessica curled into a ball as she screamed, keeping her eyes tightly shut. She felt the car jerk again as Nora fired her gun. More gunfire sounded from outside and more glass showered down on her. She heard Nora scream and felt the car jerk again, then heard the tearing screech of metal on metal as the police car crashed into the guard rail and ground to a stop.

Jessica opened her eyes and turned to look at Nora, broken glass tumbling off her head as she did so. Nora was covered in blood. "Oh my God!" Jessica breathed as she rose to a sitting position. Then a gloved hand snaked in through the shattered window behind her and tangled in her hair and jerked her back out the window.

Screaming in pain as she was hauled bodily out the window by her hair, Jessica saw two large men in military style clothes before the hand let go of her hair and a black bag was dragged down over her head. She felt herself lifted into the air and carried a short distance, then she was tossed into a vehicle and the doors slammed closed. It was too much. Jessica Monroe closed her eyes and passed into oblivion.

Chapter Fourteen

They were pulling up in front of the police station when the dispatcher came across the radio that a 911 call had come in about a police car crashing and a bunch of men in military uniforms pulling a woman out of the car and driving off. An ambulance was already on the way to the scene.

"That had to be Nora's car!" Monica said throwing the car into a bootleg turn and heading for Three Palms Drive.

"They didn't get Jessica without Nora putting up a fight," Decker said, his voice sounding incredibly tight to his own ears.

"The men who did this thing are walking dead men.

They just don't know it," Rafael Cortez said quietly from the back seat of Monica's car.

"You got that right!" Monica Sinclair hissed through tightly clenched teeth. Decker glanced over at her. Tears were running down her cheeks.

"Don't worry, Monica, we're going to get these fuckers," Decker said quietly.

Rufus Drake was already on the scene, along with Jill Bertram, both directing traffic around the scene and setting up crime scene tape to close off the lanes where debris lay spread across the asphalt. An Ambulance was sitting across two lanes of traffic and the paramedics already had Nora Santiago out of the car and on the gurney and were busy securing her to it and trying to stabilize her condition. Monica skidded her car to a halt and was outside running for the ambulance almost before the car had quit moving.

"She drives like a mad woman," Cortez shuddered as he climbed out of the back seat.

"Right now she is a mad woman," Decker shut his door and started walking towards the ambulance.

"You suspected something like this might happen," Cortez said softly.

"I thought it might. That's why I didn't let Tanner come with us," Decker nodded.

"You think he called these guys in?" Cortez stopped moving.

"I don't know, Rafe. I think maybe it's a question that we'll be asking him the next time we see him," Decker turned and started walking again. Decker hoped that he was wrong about Tanner; that the man hadn't been corrupted by working side by side with Benny the Jet.

The doors were closing on the ambulance as he and Rafael reached it. Monica stood silently watching as the driver climbed in and headed for the hospital. "She may not make it, Nora was hit pretty hard," Monica said very softly.

"I'll call Diego," Decker offered.

"That's my job," Monica shook her head.

"Your job is to go to the hospital and be there when Nora comes out of surgery," Decker took her in his arms and held her as Monica broke into body wrenching sobs. Nora was the first of her officers to be injured in the line of duty. Decker knew how she felt. He had felt the same way when he had seen that impossible name in the ledger at the Marina. Benny the Jet. It had to be. This time, Benny wasn't going to slide. And if Tanner proved to be involved, he would die as well.

*****

Jessica Monroe curled into a fetal position in the back seat of what she guessed was one of the large black SUV's that had crashed Nora Santiago's police car. The men that had taken her didn't speak. There was only silence in the car except for the rush of wind through the open windows.

She could smell sweat and body odor and the coppery scent of her own fear. They had made no effort to search her for the disc and she still had her purse. She wondered if they were after her for some other purpose than recovering the computer disc. Could Antonio have found her at last? She shivered at the thought, remembering how the mobster had sworn he would kill her someday. Could that day have finally come?

Jessica forced the thought away. Fear of her past would do nothing to help her in her present situation. She had to focus on a way to get loose, free of her present circumstances. She needed to calm herself. Calm her self and wait for the perfect opportunity.

*****

"According to the witnesses, two black SUV's forced Nora's car into the railing, shooting at it. Nora bless her heart, was returning fire when she was hit. Finally they got the car stopped and men in military fatigues dragged Jessica Monroe out of the car, pulled a black cloth bag over her head, forced her into their vehicle and drove off," Jill Bertram shrugged. Her eyes looked haunted as she had given her report. Decker could certainly understand why.

"You did a good job taking that statement. Wait on Tom and Gina to get here to start processing the scene, then I want you to head right to the station and write up the witness statements and the report. Make sure you include everything you told me," Decker reached over and patted her on the shoulder. He wondered if this would make Jill rethink her career in law enforcement and quit, or if she would stay with it.

He desperately wanted to call Monica to find out how Nora was doing, but knew that it was too soon to know anything. By now she had called Diego and he was on his way to the hospital to await news about his wife. Decker was suddenly glad he wasn't there to see Diego's reaction to the news that his beloved wife had been shot.

"What now, Jefe?" Cortez asked quietly. Only someone who didn't know Rafael Cortez would not realize how angry he was. On the surface, he appeared very calm and still, yet Decker could sense his friend's outrage over what had happened to Nora. He still hadn't figured out what the connection was between the two of them, but it was a close connection. He had never seen Cortez so upset.

*****

"Where is she, Benito? Where have you taken her?" his boss asked.

"Navarro has her. He and his men hit the transport just a short time ago. She's been taken to the safehouse until we can get the plane in to pick them up and bring them to you in Miami," Benny the Jet replied nervously.

"Does she have the disc?" his boss asked quietly.

"She does. Navarro had the phone tapped of the police woman that she was staying with. She has the disc, she was taking it to Decker," Benny wiped the sweat from his brow. Even speaking on the telephone, Benny was smart enough to be afraid of the man on the other end. He had connections that Benny could never hope to fathom.

"Decker's usefulness has ended. Kill him and bring the woman to me," the voice commanded.

"Gladly," Benny the Jet felt himself smile as he broke the connection. Sam Decker was about to die. He had been wanting to kill the bastard for years.

*****

Sam Decker called a taxi to pick up Cortez and

take him back to the Parrot's Beak to get his car. Cortez
would come back to get him. Then they would be off to
visit Mama Celeste to ask her about Benny. He knew that
Mama Celeste made Rafael nervous but again he wasn't
sure why. There seemed to be a lot he didn't know about
this case and it was starting to aggravate the shit out of him.

Decker walked the skid marks from where Nora's
car had been run off the road and into the guardrail. He
knelt down as he spotted a piece of brass from one of
the rounds that had been fired. It was unusually big. He
slipped a pen from his pocket and used it to pick up the
shell casing, lifting it up so he could check the footplate.

"Shit," he stood. No wonder Nora had been hit
hard. It was a .50 caliber pistol cartridge. Somebody had
been loaded for fucking bear. He felt his lips twitch into
a grin. Little Nora had put up a hell of a fight. Enough
of one for the kidnappers to have pulled out the heavy
artillery. "Good for you, Nora," he whispered. Decker
returned the casing to its original position and called Tom
Ortiz over to mark it and photograph it.

Decker stood and pulled out his phone dialing the
number from memory. "Lincoln," announced a voice at the
other end of the connection.

"Tell me who working the Central American circuit

uses a .50 autoloader. There can't be that many guys big enough to handle something that large," Decker said.

"Ah Samuel. How goes your retirement to the obscure little island in the Keys?" Devon Lincoln asked. Lincoln was an employee of the Central Intelligence Agency on the Central and South American desks. He and Decker had been friends for years, ever since Decker had saved his life in Columbia on a joint CIA/DEA operation.

"It goes well, Devon. Right now I'm working as a homicide consultant for the Scorpion Cay Police Department. One of the officers was shot when a witness she was driving to the station was kidnapped. The shooter used a .50," Decker walked along the skid marks, searching for other casings.

"Give me a bit to run it and I'll call you back. I assume you have the same mobile number," Lincoln replied. Decker could hear the tapping of a keyboard over the connection.

"I do," Decker replied then he flipped the phone closed. He heard a horn honk and looked up. Rafael was parked just on the other side of the tape, waiting for him with his flashers blinking. Decker walked over and opened the door and slid into the car. The Silver Mercedes slipped back into traffic.

"Where to, Jefe?" Cortez asked, flipping the radio to a Salsa station.

"We go see Mama Celeste," Decker took out a cigarette and fired it up.

"Do you have to smoke in my car?" Cortez sighed, hitting a button and dropping Decker's window down. The smoke was drawn out into the slipstream.

"I need to think. It helps," Decker shrugged, blowing out some smoke.

"You need to quit those things, Decker. Otherwise, someday they are going to kill you," Cortez shook his head.

"Probably," Decker shrugged again. He almost had it down to an art form. The rest of the ride to the Marina was made in silence except for the music blaring from the radio. Finally Cortez turned into the gravel parking lot and guided the car to a stop in front of the wood and bamboo shack where Mama Celeste did business. Decker got out of the car.

"You coming?" Decker asked, leaning back into the car to look at his friend.

"Is it necessary?" Cortez asked, tension in his voice.

"It might be. We need answers. Sometimes you are better at getting them than I am," Decker grinned.

"You are such a pain in the ass, Decker," Cortez

grumbled as he climbed out of the car.

"I try," Decker grinned. Together they walked to the door. Today the shack was quiet, not at all like it had been the night before when the drums were going and he had found a dead Treasury Agent. Decker was just about to knock when the door swung open.

"Enter," Mama Celeste called from the other side of the room.

"Bad idea," Cortez shook his head.

"C'mon you big baby," Decker nodded his head and walked inside. He looked at the old woman sitting in the cane chair on the other side of the room. "One of these days, Mama, I'll figure out how you do that," Decker flashed her his biggest smile.

"No you won't Sammy because you don' really believe," Mama said chuckling. "You ain't like Rafe dere; he knows de power of de spirit world."

"Priestess," Cortez said, bowing slightly in a gesture of respect.

"No need for formalities, Boy. Just call me Mama like Ol' Sammy here."

"Mama, can you help us find Benito Juarez?" Decker asked.

"You step careful, Sammy. De Baron he be walkin'

on your shadow. Rafael, you stay close to dis foolish white boy. He's messing wit' some bad juju," Mama said fixing her gaze on Cortez.

"Yes, Mama," Cortez nodded respectfully. Mama Celeste turned her attention back to Decker.

"What you want dat fool Benny for?" she asked puffing on her pipe.

"He's tied into the murder of Russell Cosgrove somehow. And I think he's behind the kidnapping of Jessica Monroe," Decker shrugged as if it were nothing out of the ordinary. However where Mama Celeste was concerned, he had no idea what ordinary might be.

"He also tied in wit' the men dat shot your sister," Mama fixed her good eye on Cortez once more. Decker saw him stiffen with shock, but other than that he had no reaction. "She gone be okay. She a strong woman, Rafael and she got a good man dat love her. He take good care of her."

"Mama, where is Benny?" Decker asked softly.

"He holed up out on Skull Point. You be careful though. Him surrounded by a lot of really bad men.

"Thanks, Mama," Decker said, dropping a twenty into a can near the door as he and Cortez left.

Chapter Fifteen

"Nora Santiago is your sister," Decker said as the Mercedes speed towards Skull Point.

"Yes. I tried to keep my distance from her due to our lines of work, but it isn't always easy," Rafael replied shifting.

"So Cortez is her maiden name," Decker said.

"What's in a name, Jefe?" Cortez asked.

"Nothing really," Decker replied.

"It's not something either of us advertise. Diego knows. Now you know. What I don't understand is how that spooky old woman knew," Rafael shook his head as he sent the car speeding across the island. Skull Point was on the southern tip. It was so named because a bunch of skulls from the seventeen hundreds had unearthed there many years ago.

"How you want to do this?" Decker asked, drawing his pistol and making sure the magazine was full and there was a live round under the hammer.

"We go in shooting. It's the only way to be sure," Cortez had turned off the radio.

"What about Jessica?" Decker shot Cortez a look.

"We hope she's smart enough to hit the floor and stay out of the line of fire," Rafael's voice was so soft Decker could barely hear it over the rush of wind through the windows. Decker's cell phone started to ring. He dug it out of his pocket and flipped it open. "Decker."

"Samuel, I have a name for you," Devon Lincoln's voice announced in his ear.

"Great work, Lincoln. What's the name?" Decker felt his heart rate climb a little in anticipation.

"Eduardo Navarro. He usually works with a hand-picked four man team. That big .50 handgun is his signature weapon, Samuel. Be careful. Navarro is extremely dangerous," Lincoln replied.

"So am I Lincoln," Decker shrugged. "Any idea who he might be working for?"

"Not us. After some debacle in Argentina there is now a shoot on sight order for him issued by no less than the director of operations himself," Lincoln added.

"So if I kill him, it will give me some leverage on the agency," Decker asked, wanting clarification.

"I would never suggest such a thing, Samuel, but in a word, yes," Lincoln replied.

"Talk to you later, Lincoln," Decker flipped the phone closed with a smile. "Hey Rafe, you ever hear of a guy named Ed Navarro?"

"Yeah, he's a mercenary usually works down south," Cortez replied.

"According to a source at Langley, he's the one that shot Nora. The news gets better though. The CIA wants him hit," Decker grinned.

"That is good news," Cortez smiled. Decker shuddered. Right now, the smile on Rafael's face reminded him too much of skin stretched too tightly over the bone.

*****

Monica stood near the door of the surgical waiting room. It seemed like hours had passed since Nora had been shot. Hours since they had wheeled her straight from the emergency room to a surgical theater. Monica downed the rest of her coffee. Was it her third cup or fourth? She couldn't remember.

Monica reached up and ran her fingers through her long blonde hair, pushing it back out of her face. Diego sat impassively against the wall in one of the uncomfortable plastic chairs that reminded her of a high school lunch room. His hands moved constantly in his lap and it took her a moment to realize that he was praying and saying a rosary, asking that his wife be healed and would live. It had been years since she had prayed about anything. Maybe it was time. Monica dropped to her knees and folded her hands and she began to pray.

*****

"Give me the disc," a soft yet menacing man's voice almost whispered in her ear. Jessica Monroe opened her eyes and slowly sat up. The man that had spoken to her was well over six feet tall, his skin burned to a dark brown by constant exposure to tropical sun. His dark hair was streaked white.

"Who are you?" she asked, emboldened by the fact that they had yet to abuse her in any way.

"Names are not important, Chiquita. What do you care about names?" the obvious leader of the group asked.

"I don't really. However I need to call you something," she smiled. The man nodded his head as if it had been understood all along.

"No you needn't call me anything. As long as I continue to treat you well, you should be thanking me," Ed laughed.

"Why is that?" Jessica looked into his eyes as she asked the question.

"Well, for starters our good friend Benny over there, he wanted to just shoot you and be done with it. However the Boss has other ideas. When the plane gets here, we will be flying to Miami so that the Boss can question you about the disc himself," Ed smiled, revealing even white teeth that contrasted sharply with his dark brown skin.

"Why do you want the disc?" Jessica asked lifting her head slightly.

"Because knowledge is power. My employer wants this disc badly, so there must be a reason for it. If I can profit from that reason, so much the better," Ed threw back his head and laughed.

"Eduardo, you talk too much," Benito Juarez called from the other side of the room.

"Fool!" the man now identified as Eduardo spun towards the man Jessica presumed was Benny, his gun out of its holster and leveled at Benny's head. "Benny you know better than to call me by name. Perhaps I should go ahead and end your involvement now."

"You worry too much. She won't be around to identify you after the Boss is done with her," Benny waved one hand lazily in front of him.

"So you say, but how do I know, eh?" Ed asked, his smile returning. He gestured to one of the other men and nodded towards Benny," If he moves, kill him."

*****

Monica looked up as a tired looking man wearing green scrubs emerged from the swinging double doors and then stopped, looking around the room. She climbed to her feet. "How is she?" Monica asked as Diego suddenly stood as well.

"Mrs. Santiago is a fighter. She came through the surgery well and should have a full recovery," the surgeon grinned.

"Thank God," Monica said, grabbing Diego and hugging him with all her strength.

*****

Rafael Cortez rolled his Mercedes quietly to a halt behind a stand of trees. He and Decker were both out of the car almost before it had stopped moving. Cortez was holding and M-16/M-205 assault rifle/ grenade launcher combination. A fifty-round drum was loaded into the assault rifle, and a 40mm High Explosive Grenade was loaded into the short wide tube below the rifle barrel.

Decker carried a Heckler & Koch MP-5 submachine gun with two thirty round magazines attached to each other with a double clip. His Trusty old Browning Hi-Power was tucked into a shoulder holster beneath his left armpit. Decker motioned for Cortez to wait as he began working his way towards the back of the small bungalow through the trees.

Decker knew that Rafael would open the dance very quickly and in a most deadly fashion. He wanted to be in position when it happened so that he might have a better chance of getting Jessica Monroe out alive. As he moved past the back corner of the house, he caught a movement from the corner of his eye. Decker spun toward the movement, his finger squeezing the trigger of the silenced MP-5, firing off a short 3-round burst that dropped a man in military fatigues to the sand behind the house. Decker moved out of the trees, moving closer to the house. Just then a ball of fire erupted from the front of the house.

As the rear glass door slid open, Decker grinned. Rafe always had been good at getting folks attention. Two of the fatigue-clad men ran outside and he cut them down with two short bursts from the MP-5. A large caliber handgun boomed and a branch exploded from a tree near him, sending him diving to the sand as another bullet whistled over his head. The chatter of M-16 fire tore through the afternoon air followed by a scream. Decker saw a male form dart from the house and head for the beach even as the sound of a plane's engine reached his ears.

Decker pushed to his feet as he recognized Benny the Jet and started after him. Behind him he could hear the loud booming report of a very large caliber handgun, then the chatter of the M-16 again. There was another explosion, then silence from behind him. Decker dismissed it, concentrating on the running figure of Benny the Jet and the rapidly approaching plane engine.

Benny had left the beach and was up to his waist in the surf as Decker emerged on the beach. An amphibious plane was dipping down towards the water as Decker raised the MP-5 and fired at the plane, causing it to turn and rise into the air. A bullet whipped past his head and Decker spun towards the water once more, squeezing the trigger.

Benny the Jet screamed as bullets tore into his chest and spun him around into an oncoming wave. Decker watched in satisfaction as Benny slid beneath the waves. Smiling he turned and walked back towards the house, the H&K subgun at the ready.

Rafael Cortez was standing behind what was left of the house with Jessica Monroe. Jessica smiled when she saw him and Decker felt a twinge of guilt. Jessica was an absolute drop dead gorgeous beauty, and looked like she could be very grateful for her rescue. However, he had Monica to think about. He liked her, liked her a lot. Jessica would be nice, but Monica might be permanent if he played his cards right. For once in his life, Decker decided to go with permanent.

*****

Mitch Tanner and Monica Sinclair were both waiting for them when the three of them arrived at the station. Diego had already called Rafael and told him that Nora would live and likely be none the worse for her ordeal. Cortez had told Diego that the men responsible for what had happened to Nora were dead. Diego had seemed relieved.

"So what happened?" Monica asked after the five of them had all sat down.

"Benny the Jet is dead," Decker replied, leaning back in his seat.

"I'll believe that when I see a body," Tanner shook his head.

"He took a whole clip from a submachine gun in the chest from less than twenty yards and then his body washed out with the tide," Decker shrugged.

"The mercenaries that had kidnapped Miss Monroe are also dead," Cortez added with a smile.

"Do we know who killed Russell Cosgrove?" Monica asked.

"Not exactly. However we do know who ordered his death and why," Decker shrugged once more.

"You really like to keep us in suspense, don't you?" Monica smiled.

"Of course. It's so much fun," Decker grinned.

"Spill it," Monica ordered, rising to her feet.

"Jason Marshall was using Delacorte Enterprises to launder money that didn't come from Miguel Delacorte. He was also embezzling money from Contras Enterprises and using it to build up his own portfolio. Russell discovered a paper trail and planned on hiring me to follow it. Except Marshall realized that Cosgrove was on to him and he hired a hitman to take Russell out. My guess is that Benny was the actual hitter, though how he made it back to Miami in time to catch the chopper out is anybody's guess," Decker explained.

"And that would certainly explain why the boys

from the Treasury Department were looking at the law firm rather than the merger itself," Tanner nodded.

"Exactly. I figure Benny must have hired a local to snuff the T-man at Mama Celeste's house to try and keep himself free of the federal investigation.," Decker stood and paced the room.

"That would certainly explain a lot," Monica nodded.

"Russell had made a list of times, names and dates and burned them onto a CD. He then hid it among the back-up discs I had for my novel," Jessica added.

"So basically, all the bad guys were working for Marshall," Tanner said, asking for clarification.

"He's quick for a state cop," Cortez grinned.

"Sometimes he even makes sense," Decker grinned.

*****

Samuel Decker rolled off of Monica Sinclair. His lips tasted of her sweat when he kissed her, the slightly salty tang a wonderful taste upon his lips. A ceiling fan spun silently overhead, cooling them after a particularly long and arduous session of love-making.

"How did you know it was Marshall?" Monica sat up and reached for a pack of cigarettes from the nightstand.

"Process of elimination. Plus, he had no real reason

to go and search the house unless he had something to hide," Decker shrugged.

"Plus with Cosgrove gone, he moved up a notch at the law firm," Monica nodded.

"Exactly. It gave him everything he wanted. Access to high-paying clients, drugs, and money," Decker nodded.

"How did he take it when Tanner arrested him?" Monica rolled over on her side and propped her head up on one hand.

"About like you'd expect. He screamed for a bloody attorney at the top of his fucking lungs. Funny thing, nobody at his firm would have anything to do with his defense," Decker grinned.

"So where does that leave us?" Monica grinned.

"Only time will tell," Decker grinned, then he kissed her hard on the lips, silencing off anything he had to say.

Sam Decker will return in

Killshot!